TAKE THE LONG WAY HOME

BRIAN KEENE

deadite
press

DEADITE PRESS
205 NE BRYANT
PORTLAND, OR 97217
www.DEADITEPRESS.com

AN ERASERHEAD PRESS COMPANY
www.ERASERHEADPRESS.com

"Take the Long Way Home" first appeared as a limited edition hardback
by Necessary Evil Press in 2006.

ISBN: 1-936383-48-9

Acknowledgments: For this new edition of *Take The Long Way Home*, my thanks to everyone at Deadite Press; Alan Clark; Joe Nassise, Gord Rollo, Tim Lebbon, and Michael Laimo (for the origin of this novella); John Skipp; Nick Kaufmann; Mary SanGiovanni; and my sons.

For my parents, Lloyd and Shannon Keene, with love, respect and admiration.

DEADITE PRESS BOOKS BY BRIAN KEENE
Urban Gothic
Jack's Magic Beans
Clickers II (with J. F. Gonzalez)
Take The Long Way Home
A Gathering of Crows

Author's Note

Although many of the exits and locations in this novella exist alongside Interstate 83 as it carves its way through Pennsylvania and Maryland, I have taken certain fictional liberties with them. Don't look for them during your daily commute. They might have vanished along with everyone else.

PEELING THE SKIN OFF OF GOD'S KNUCKLE SANDWICH, ONE PUNCH TO THE TEETH AT A TIME

AN INTRODUCTION BY JOHN SKIPP

Let's face it: life is a bastard sometimes. It will sneak up behind you and kick your ass. It will spin you around and smack you right in the face, then jab you quick in the solar plexus; and as you whoof with pain, doubling over by reflex, it will bring its knee up to shatter your nose.

You stagger back, squirting, and life moves in for the kill: a professional of such infinite experience that it seems almost bored as it takes you apart.

If you get whacked around like that enough—and you happen to believe in God—then you might start to wonder, "What is WRONG with that guy? Is He some kind of crazed bully? Is He off of his meds?

"WHAT THE FUCK IS THE MATTER WITH HIM?"

Sure, if you're big on passing the buck, you can blame it all on Satan. But WHO HIRED SATAN? In life—if you've been around the block more than once—you can almost always trace the muscle back to the source by following the money.

Or you can blame it on yourself. Which is a good idea, when you're actually responsible . . . but not quite as easy to swallow when you're just minding your own business, trying to be cool, and suddenly life/God/Satan/whatever sneaks up and kicks the living shit out of you.

Now, for all too many of us, the natural response to an onslaught by overwhelming odds is to curl up, protect the most vulnerable areas, and pray to God that we survive.

If we live through it—and we always do, till the day we don't—we are also left to puzzle out why this is happening to us. Why this is happening at all.

But have you ever watched a good human being get hammered, over and over, and yet stubbornly REFUSE TO FALL?

It's an amazing sight. It happens all too rarely. It's gladiator shit, on the most meaningful scale: a strength of character, a firmness of resolve, and a love of the best, most meaningful parts of life that is SO STRONG, and SO TRUE, that it takes every punch to the face it gets handed.

Swings back, with all of its might.

And keeps swinging, even as it gets pummeled to its knees.

That doesn't stop till it can swing no more.

And, even then, wills its arm up for one more blow.

This isn't just testosterone and feisty DNA.

This is a heart on fire.

Which brings me, at last, to the writer in question, and the book you're about to read.

Brian Keene's prose has a firm handshake. That was one of the first things I noticed. It's strong, and direct, and personable, like the guy who stands behind it. He doesn't try to dazzle you with wordplay. He doesn't feint and weave. For him, this fight is not polite. And there is neither place nor patience for bullshit.

Keene shakes your hand, then wades right in: a no-nonsense literary slugger with a keen wit, tremendous endurance, and a great sense of detail and rhythm and pacing. He places his blows just so, landing them right where he knows they'll hurt, or surprise you with a simple, perfect, beautiful truth.

I've only read three of his books so far—*The Rising, Terminal,* and the one before you—and if there's one thread I've noted throughout, it's an astounding *resolve*: defiance coupled with an absolute determination to see this through. A demand for understanding. And a deep, deep yearning for nothing less.

So that peace can be found.

So that peace can be earned.

I respect the fuck out of that.

In fact, I respect the fuck out of my man Keene, pretty much across the board. He's one of the hardest-workin' boyz in the biz (Go ahead! Ask him about his *next twelve books!*); and as a stand-up guy in a curled-up world, he's uniquely great at galvanizing the literary troops, getting them up off their asses. I love to watch him work the horror crowd. It is, in a word, inspiring.

One of the great delights of my career has been meeting the generation of writers I inspired: amazing guys like Brian Keene, Cody Goodfellow, and Carlton Mellick III (name-checked herein, in a wacky cameo). It makes me especially proud, because these cats are The Real Deal. If my shit helped, then—gulp—*God bless me!*

I gotta say, though, that Keene is the one clearly emerging new rock star of horror, insofar as I'm concerned. If his books were music, they would occupy a working class, hard-earned space on the shelf between Springsteen, Eminem, and Johnny Cash (not surprisingly, three of his heroes). His edges are raw, his emotions are pure, and his grooves throb with the oftentimes-spilled, still heart-pulsing blood of the ages.

That said, this isn't a big-ass rock star turn. It's more like Springsteen's *Nebraska*, maybe gene-spliced a little with King's *The Long Walk*: a whisper of godforsaken highway, wind whistling through the holes in a shattered acoustic guitar.

No zombies. No giant earthworms.

Just us, and our destiny.

And a punch in the teeth.

DOES GOD FEEL OUR PAIN? If It does, *It is feeling this book, right now.*

Going "OW," as the skin scrapes off Its knuckles.

Maybe even questioning, for a moment, Its plan.

Or, at least, in awe—as I am—of anyone who stands up.

And takes a bite out of the fist that feeds them.

John Skipp
Just outside of L.A.
December, 2005

1

I kept my eyes shut after the blast. My head was throbbing and blood filled my mouth. Wincing at the taste, I explored with my tongue and found that I'd bitten the inside of my cheek—probably on impact.

"Steve?"

Charlie. It sounded like he was in pain.

"Steve, you okay?"

I opened my eyes and blinked, staring at the dent my head had made in the dashboard. I spat, bright red, and then spat again. There were chunks of broken glass in my lap, and I wondered where they'd come from. Then it all came rushing back to me.

"Yeah," I groaned. "I'm okay. How about you?"

Charlie coughed. "Got the wind knocked out of me, but I'm alright. What the hell happened?"

I didn't answer, because the answer was obvious. We'd wrecked. It had all happened so suddenly. We'd just gotten out of work, and were crawling north on Interstate 83 during Baltimore's evening rush hour. Hector was behind the wheel, cursing in Spanish because we'd just been funneled from four lanes down to two, and wondering why they couldn't do road construction at night, after the rush hour was over. I rode shotgun, staring out the window at nothing and everything, watching the trees and buildings and road signs flash by, and half-listening to NPR's *All Things Considered*. Even though it was Hector's van, we took turns with the radio each day. He liked the Spanish station, I preferred classic rock, and Craig and Charlie both liked National Public Radio. But Craig and Charlie weren't listening to the radio. They were in the backseat, arguing over the Ravens' chances of making the Super Bowl this year, which according to Charlie were great, and according to Craig were slim to none and slim had just left town.

I'd opened my mouth to warn Hector that the yuppie idiot driving the Volvo in front of us was gabbing on his cell phone and not paying attention to the road—but I never got the chance.

Because of that weird fucking blast.

It wasn't an explosion. Didn't sound like that at all. What it sounded like was a trumpet. The world's biggest trumpet, blaring a single, concussive, ear-splitting note. I felt it in my chest when it went off, the impact vibrating my ribs. I hadn't seen any smoke or fire. No mushroom clouds on the horizon. No airplanes slamming into buildings or box trucks blowing up on the median strip. None of the usual things you think of these days when you hear a blast.

It must have startled Hector. He jumped in his seat and jerked the steering wheel hard. At the same time, the Volvo darted in front of a flatbed truck loaded down with huge steel pipes for a construction site. The truck swerved into our lane to avoid the Volvo, and we sideswiped a concrete construction barrier. The van came to a sudden, jarring stop. My teeth ground together. The air bags deployed on impact. I'd blacked out for a minute or two.

And now here we were.

I spat blood again.

Charlie moaned in the back seat. "This is fucked up."

I didn't respond. Each time I talked, I swallowed more blood. My stomach felt queasy. Unfastening my seatbelt, I brushed fragments of glass from my hair and lap, and turned towards Hector. My mouth fell open and blood dribbled down my chin.

"Oh fuck . . ."

There was a pipe jutting from his head. His eyes, nose, and mouth were gone, just eradicated, replaced with a twelve-inch round length of steel pipe. My gaze followed the pipe's trajectory: from the ruined thing that used to be Hector's face to the windshield, over the hood, and into the back of the flatbed truck. An old elementary school rhyme ran through my head: *Through the teeth and over the gums, look out stomach—here it comes.* My mind then changed it to: *Through the windshield and past your gums, look out Hector—here it comes.* I gave a nervous little laugh. The sound scared me.

"Steve?" Charlie's voice was concerned. It must have scared him, too.

Sour bile rose in my throat, and my stomach lurched. I touched Hector's bloody shoulder and gave him a gentle shake. It was a stupid thing to do, but the mind is funny that way in times of crisis. Hector didn't move. His arms hung limp. There was an ugly splotch on his wrist where the airbag had burned him.

"Is he okay?" Charlie asked.

"Take a look. What do you think?"

Somewhere behind us, a car horn blared, loud and obnoxious. I checked Hector's pulse, but there was none. I'd expected as much, but I went through the motions anyway. My own heartbeat quickened. I couldn't put my fingers under his nose to determine if he was breathing, because he didn't have a nose anymore. He had a pipe instead. And besides, he wasn't breathing anyway.

Abruptly, the car horn died.

"He's gone." The words caught in my throat. The whole situation seemed surreal.

"Jesus Christ." Charlie undid his seatbelt and leaned forward, pressing on my seat. "We've got to do CPR on him or something! Use your cell phone. Call 911, man."

"I don't think that's going to help him, Charlie. He's dead."

"But—"

"He's fucking dead, man! He's got no face. He's got no fucking face…"

"Well, how could this happen? I mean, we were only doing what, forty-five miles an hour? Maybe? The airbags deployed."

"Yeah. But he's got a pipe sticking out of his head. It punched right through the air bag and into his head. His face is gone."

Charlie's response was a choked half-sob, half-sigh.

"Are you hurt?" I asked.

"I don't think so." He rustled around in the backseat and

15

then paused. "Where's Craig?"

"He's not back there?" I whipped around, and immediately wished that I hadn't. The muscles in my neck and shoulders screamed.

"Do you see him back here, Steve?"

"Check the cargo space behind you."

"I did. I'm telling you, man. He's not in here!"

My eyes darted around the van's interior, trying to confirm this new bit of information. There were no Craig-sized holes in the side door or back windshield. The roof and floor were intact. The doors were closed. But there was no sign of Craig.

"Shit." I pressed my face into my palms, trying to hold back the sudden and severe headache blossoming behind my eyes. "He must have been thrown from the vehicle. Come on. We've got to find him."

Charlie blinked, and I noticed that his pupils were dilated. They looked like two black blobs of India ink. He grabbed my arm. His hands were sweaty.

"Steve, the only hole is the one in the windshield. Where the pipe is. He couldn't have been thrown out."

I shook him off and opened the passenger door. Hot steam rose from the engine, smearing the windows, and I breathed in a lungful. I stumbled out onto the highway, coughing and gagging.

Charlie followed. He leaned against the side of the van, his eyes wide and dazed. "We were only doing forty-five. We were only doing forty-fucking-five."

I got the impression that he was repeating the mantra in an effort to bring back Hector and Craig, as if verifying the safety of our speed would rewind the past two minutes. I reached for him. The ground seemed to spin and I fought to keep my balance. My legs suddenly felt like they were made of rubber. My ears rang, and I started sweating. I could feel it pouring off my forehead and pooling beneath my arms. Charlie said something, but it sounded like he was talking from the end of a very long tunnel. My vision dimmed.

Shock, I thought. *You're going into shock. It's okay, Steve-O. You were just banged around in an automobile accident, and one of your co-workers has been killed—he*

16

has a pipe in his face—and another one is missing. You're allowed to go into shock if you want to. Nobody will mind. Go right ahead. Hector will still be dead when you wake up.

I tried to speak. "Charlie—"

"Yeah?"

The road fell out from under me, and I dropped. Then God turned off the lights, and I blacked out again. I'm not sure how long I was out. Probably only a few seconds, but it seemed like hours.

When I opened my eyes, the first thing I was aware of was being thirsty. My mouth was dry, my tongue swollen. The second thing was that Charlie and two strangers were leaning over me. One was a black man in a neatly pressed white shirt and tie with a cross on it. I remember noticing his attire right away—end of the workday and this guy's shirt still looked freshly ironed. Pants creased. Tie smooth, unwrinkled. He looked *crisp*. His wiry goatee and mustache were peppered with silver hairs, and when he smiled his teeth gleamed white. The other man was an overweight white guy in a yellow hardhat and flannel shirt. Underneath the flannel was a stained wife-beater T-shirt, stretched over his prodigious belly. His nose and ruddy face were lined with the red veins of advanced alcoholism. His armpits reeked, and thick beads of sweat rolled off his cheeks.

All three of them leaned close, staring at me in concern. I could smell the horseradish from the sandwich Charlie had eaten for lunch.

"What?" I smacked my lips together, trying to work up enough spit to talk. My mouth felt like cotton.

"You okay?" Charlie's brow creased.

I nodded, so that I wouldn't have to talk. My hands hurt and I raised my palms to investigate. They were bleeding, cut by the small stones in the asphalt.

"Just lie still, buddy," the guy wearing the hardhat said. "I called 911 on my cell phone. Cops and an ambulance are on the way."

I turned back to Charlie. "Craig?"

He shook his head. "I can't find him. And nobody saw him get thrown from the vehicle, either."

17

I thought about this, turning it over in my mind. It didn't make sense. Where had he gone? Craig couldn't have just wandered away—Charlie had remained conscious immediately after the crash, and I'd only been out for a few seconds. We would have known if Craig had climbed from the van. He hadn't. And he wasn't inside the van either.

So where the hell was he?

Charlie glanced around, looking nervous and frightened. I wondered if there was something he wasn't telling me.

I struggled to sit up, but the black man pushed me back down. His touch was light, but powerful. It felt like all the strength in the world was in those warm hands. A small jolt of static electricity shot from his fingertips to my chest.

"Easy now." His voice was like flowing water. "Just rest until the paramedics get here."

My head still throbbed, but my saliva was working again and I managed to speak. "You are?"

He smiled. "Gabriel. Or Gabe. Whichever you prefer. I caught you as you fell."

"Not quick enough, though," the man in the hardhat grunted. "You scraped your hands."

I tried to sit up again, but Gabriel gently forced me back down. "Just lie still."

"I'm okay," I insisted. "We need to find our friend. And our other co-worker, Hector, he's . . ."

I trailed off, unwilling to finish the sentence. Could Hector really be dead? It just didn't seem possible. Earlier in the day, Charlie and I had stood in his cubicle, laughing over a dirty cartoon Hector downloaded off the Internet. In it, the cast of *Family Guy* was having sex with *The Simpsons*. We hadn't shown it to Craig, of course. He was our friend, but he was also a born-again Christian, and we didn't want to offend him. Craig wasn't preachy. In fact, he didn't bring God up unless somebody asked him directly. He respected our views (I was Jewish and Charlie was agnostic; said he couldn't worship a God who'd condemn him to Hell just for being gay).

We'd laughed over the cartoon. Next weekend, the four of us were going to Lake Redman for the day to do some fishing. Hector had just bought a new bass boat with his bonus. We were going to try it out. So how could Hector be dead now? It didn't make sense. And where the hell was Craig? Maybe he'd hit his head and had amnesia or something. Wandered away from the wreck.

The man in the yellow hardhat stared off into the distance. "Wonder what's taking them so long?"

"They'll be busy today," Gabriel said. "This is just the beginning."

Charlie nodded. "You heard the blast, too? Think it was terrorists?"

Gabriel didn't respond.

"Ask me, it didn't sound like no explosion," the guy in the hardhat said. "Sounded more like—well, a trumpet. Fucking weird shit."

Gabriel's smile was tight-lipped and sad. I wondered what he was thinking. Groaning, I grabbed his wrist and removed his hand from my chest. Then I sat up and spat more blood onto the pavement.

"You should rest," Gabriel said again, rising to his feet. "You're going to need it before this day is through, Steven, and I will be very busy with other things. I won't be able to catch you again if you fall."

"What?"

I wondered how he knew my name. Before I could ask, my attention was drawn to the crowd. They were all around us, people from all walks of life. Bankers, customer service representatives, cabbies, stockbrokers, IT techs, secretaries, construction workers, janitors, telemarketers, forklift drivers, systems analysts, machine operators, and soccer moms, all stranded together in the middle of the interstate during Wednesday afternoon's rush hour. We saw each other every day, drove past one another, competed against each other for lane supremacy, shouted at each other and flashed obscene finger gestures when we lost. But none of us had ever truly met, until now. It was like some bizarre version of *The Breakfast Club*.

Charlie gave me his sweaty hand and pulled me to my feet. He squeezed, forgetting about my cut palms.

"Ouch." Wincing, I pulled my hand away.

He wiped my blood on his slacks. "Sorry, dude."

"That's okay. Listen, did you tell that guy my name?"

"Who?" Charlie looked confused.

"The black guy. Gabriel."

Charlie shook his head. Then he turned away and said, "God—look at this."

I glanced around, stunned by the magnitude of it all. Ours wasn't the only wreck on the highway. Remember when you were a kid, and you got out all of your Hot Wheels and Matchbox cars and made one giant traffic accident? That's what the interstate looked like. Vehicles were piled up in both directions as far as the eye could see. Some were just minor fender-benders. Other cars had been totaled. The occupants, those who were mobile at least, milled around on the median strip and weaved between the wreckage, looking as stunned as I felt. Some exchanged insurance information. Others held cell phones to their ears. Many more simply stared in shared disbelief. I wondered how many were in shock.

Charlie, the guy in the hardhat and I were standing in front of the Timonium exit. The on and off ramps were choked with snarled traffic, too. A thick forest spread out beyond the southbound lane. To our right was a steep embankment. There was a chain link fence at the bottom that surrounded a trucking company. Frantic employees ran around in the parking lot, looking as confused as we were.

A pretty redhead took a step towards us. She swallowed, made a choking noise, and then took off her shoes. I noticed that one of her heels was broken. She looked at us and said, "It's like the end of the world."

We nodded. Charlie coughed.

Then she padded away.

In the distance, a lone siren wailed.

"Sounds like the ambulance," Charlie said.

The guy in the hardhat grunted. "Guess that other fella was right. They're gonna be busy."

The siren faded. Then another one took its place.

It was mid-August and the late afternoon sun beat down on the blacktop, yet I suddenly felt very cold. Shivering, I gently rubbed my arms with my sore, bloody hands.

2

We stood there, not knowing what to do next. Charlie and I called out for Craig, but he didn't answer. In truth, I hadn't really expected him to. I glanced back at the van once, looked at Hector, and then forced myself not to look anymore.

The guy in the hardhat said nothing. I think he was too shocked to speak. He stood there and watched the employees in the parking lot of the trucking company below.

The breeze kicked up. A traffic helicopter hovered overhead, surveying the damage. Then it flew further up the highway. Some of the crowd waved their arms and hollered at it, but the chopper didn't return.

Another young woman stumbled toward us through the wreckage. She only wore one shoe. Her other foot was bare, and her nylons were torn. Her blonde hair was mussed. Tears and mascara streamed down her face along with blood from her nose.

"My baby," she sobbed. "Please, somebody help me. I can't find my baby!"

Charlie stepped forward and gently put his hands on her shoulders. "Shhhh. It'll be okay."

"Okay? My baby is missing! She's not in the car."

"Where's your vehicle?" Charlie asked, trying to calm her. "Take us to your car, and we'll help you find your daughter."

She pointed. One car behind us—an undamaged, neon green Volkswagen Jetta. There was an infant's car seat in the back. It was empty. Just like Craig's seat had been. That was when I felt the first pangs of real fear.

"Her name is Britney," the woman wailed. "I can't find her."

21

"My wife's missing," a man shouted from the opposite lane. "Has anybody seen her?"

"What's she look like?" someone else hollered.

"Brunette. Freckles. She's pregnant! We were on our way to the hospital for a check-up."

Several people clustered around him, while Charlie led the crying woman back to her car.

I thought about my own wife, Terri. No doubt the pile-up had already made the local news. She'd be worried, wondering if I was okay. I pulled out my cell phone and dialed the house. After a minute, I got a recording telling me that all lines were busy and to try my call again. Sighing in frustration, I stuffed the phone back into my pocket.

The guy in the hardhat stuck out his hand. I held up my bleeding palms and shrugged. "Sorry. Don't want to bleed on you."

"Appreciate that," he laughed. "Frank Wieczynski."

"Steve Leiberman. Nice to meet you."

He nodded. "Yeah, you too. Shame it isn't under better circumstances."

"Ain't that the truth." Cringing, I pulled a piece of gravel from my hand and smoothed a flap of loose skin over the cut. My mouth had finally quit bleeding. "Thanks for your help back there, Frank. I appreciate it. I guess it was shock or something that made me pass out like that."

He shrugged. "Don't mention it. To be honest, I didn't do much. Just called 911 as soon as the pile-up started. That's all. It was that other guy, Gabriel. He's the one you should thank. I saw him catch you when you fell. Moved like greased lightning. One second you were falling, and the next he was there, keeping you from cracking your head open on the highway."

I searched the gathering crowd, looking for Gabriel so that I could thank him, but he was gone.

"Where'd he go?" I asked.

Frank took off his hardhat and scratched his balding, sunburned head. "Don't know. He was just here a second ago."

I scanned the crowd some more, but there was no sign of him. "It's like he vanished."

"Seems to be a lot of that going on," Frank said. "Couple of other people are missing, too. Your friend over there, the one helping that blonde—he said one of your other friends was missing? That who you two were hollering for earlier?" I nodded. "Craig. He's got to be around here somewhere, though."

The yuppie from the Volvo, the one who'd been paying more attention to his cell phone than the road and had caused the truck to swerve into our lane, climbed out of his car and slammed the door. His face was like a storm cloud. Running a hand through his perfectly coifed hair, he surveyed the damage to his rear bumper, muttered something under his breath, and then glared at me. His tie fluttered in the wind. Then he turned his attention to our van, and caught sight of Hector's body. He flinched. The color drained out of his face, but he still looked angry.

"That guy still alive?" He walked over to Frank and me, one hand massaging his neck. "Because if so, then he'd better have a damn good lawyer. I think my spine is hurt."

"He's dead," I told him. "So you'll probably have to sue somebody else."

"Dead?"

"Yeah. In case you didn't notice, he's got a twelve-inch pipe sticking through his fucking face."

The Volvo driver suddenly forgot all about his supposedly injured back. "Jesus Christ. This is bullshit. I'm supposed to be in York by six. I've got a meeting."

Dismissing him with a wave of my hand, I turned back to Frank. "Is your cell phone working?"

He nodded. "Yeah. Signal was fine when I called 911. The woman said she was dispatching units right away. Sounded like she was in a hurry. Frazzled. I'll bet other people were calling about this, too."

"Maybe," I agreed. "I hate to ask, but can I borrow your phone? Mine's not working, and I'd like to call my wife. Let her know that I'm okay."

"Sure." Frank handed me his cell phone. "I'd call my old lady, but she left me two years ago."

He launched into the story, but I tuned him out, made

23

sure I had four bars on the display, and then dialed Terri. This time there was no recording. Just silence. Dead air. I waited, but there was no dial tone or ring.

"I think your cell is out of service, too." I handed the phone back to Frank.

"That's weird." He glanced at the network bars. "It worked before. Looks like I've got a signal, too."

"Maybe they're jammed up or something. Like what happened on September 11th, when everybody was trying to call home at the same time."

"Could be. If that's so, then this is even bigger than we think. That explosion was the damnedest thing. Couldn't tell where it came from exactly, but it must have been close. And I still say it sounded like a trumpet."

Before I could reply, somebody screamed nearby us. I couldn't tell if it was a man or a woman. It was just a high-pitched, drawn out wail that went on and on, and then finally faded after what seemed an eternity. A dog barked. Then another person called out, wondering where Thomas had gone. Thomas didn't answer. A small child began to cry for her mother.

Frank looked scared. "This is getting bad."

"Thomas? Thomas, you get back here, right now! Where are you?"

"Mommy? MOMMY! Where's my mommy?"

"Thomas! You quit scaring me right now. Come back."

"Motherfucker..." The guy from the Volvo threw his cell phone down, smashing it on the pavement. The broken casing slid under a nearby car. "God damn piece of shit. I've got a meeting, goddamn it!"

"That guy is losing it," I whispered to Frank.

Volvo kicked his front tire.

Frank eyed him warily. "Yeah, we'd better keep an eye on him till the cops show up."

I turned back to Charlie and the young blonde woman. She was in hysterics, crawling underneath her car and scratching at the pavement, and all the while shrieking for her missing baby. Her skirt was soiled with dirt and grease. Charlie knelt beside her, his expression a mixture of sadness and bewilderment. He looked to me for help, motioning me over.

"Leiberman," Frank grunted. "You Jewish?"

I nodded. "That's right."

"I got a friend that's a Jew. Nice guy. We play cards sometimes."

I'd heard this reaction before, many times, in fact. I guess it's that way for lots of people—white, Anglo-Saxon protestants assuring them that they have a friend who's black or Muslim or gay or Jewish, and they're okay with it. It's always struck me as sort of weird. I do know it's that way for Charlie, living as a gay man in corporate America. I've watched him go through it time and time again, usually at company functions or Christmas parties, when one of our co-workers has had too much to drink and has to prove how evolved he is by assuring Charlie that even though he's straight, he has a lot of respect for Charlie publicly admitting that he's gay. Either that, or they feel the need to list their gay friends for Charlie. I never understood the reaction, but then again, I'm not a WASP.

I wasn't dogmatic about my faith. I was Jewish by birth, rather than belief. Most of the time, I wasn't even sure if I believed in God. To be honest, the only time I really talked to Him was when I wanted something. Mine was a faith of convenience. But my parents were devout. And I'd experienced just as much intolerance from them as I had from other religions and races. More, even. Terri was a Christian—a Lutheran, just like her parents. We'd met in college. When I told my parents we were going to get married, they threw a fit, forbidding me to marry her and threatening to disown me if I went through with it. I just laughed and explained that I was an adult now, and while I loved and respected them, I could make my own decisions. Then, when they saw that I was serious, they pestered me about what faith our children would be raised in. It didn't matter to me, but my parents worried that their grandchildren wouldn't be real Jews, since Judaism is traditionally passed down through the mother's lineage. I wondered aloud if they'd love their grandchildren any less if they happened to be raised Lutheran. They didn't have an answer. I'd thought that would be the end of it. Figured they'd come to accept Terri as their daughter-in-law once we were married. But they didn't. My parents were just getting warmed up.

After the wedding, they demanded that a mezuzah be placed on the door of our house, to mark Jewish territory. Terri balked and told my mother exactly what she thought of the idea. Needless to say, relations with my family were strained from then on. I'd overheard them in private a few times, referring to Terri as a shikse. It's a term that's usually used jokingly, made popular by an old *Seinfeld* episode, but in Terri's case, they didn't mean it as a compliment.

After two years, Terri and I found out that we couldn't have children. Turned out I was sterile. Terri didn't want to adopt, and the whole point became moot anyway. Eventually, my parents dropped it.

But my heritage and our marriage didn't cause problems with just my side of the family. Terri's parents got in on the act as well, worrying about my immortal soul. Every chance they got, they'd witness to me about the glory of Christ. About how I had to be born again and needed to believe he was the son of God, that he'd died on the cross for me. And how I should ask him to come into my heart and forgive my sins, number one of which was being born into Judaism rather than Christianity. It was very important to them that I believed Jesus was the messiah. We'd had several arguments about it. At least they'd never accused me of killing their Savior. But they never missed a chance to let me know about the day when Christ would return to earth and take the faithful home. According to them, Jews—even devout ones—weren't allowed on that ride. They called it the Rapture. I'd asked Craig about it once, when we were out at a bar, and he told me that not all Christians believed in the Rapture. According to him, it wasn't even mentioned in the Bible.

Another shrieking siren brought me back to the present. Frank put his hardhat back on and stared off into the distance again. I wondered about Frank's comment. Was he secretly anti-Semitic and trying to cover it up? No, I decided. I was on edge and overreacting. It was this situation. We were standing in the midst of a massive traffic jam. Dozens of people were injured and dozens more were apparently missing. This was not a normal, everyday commute. Frank was just as scared and freaked out as I was, and he was simply trying to make conversation by telling me about his Jewish friend. I let it go, and walked towards Charlie and the woman.

"I'll see if I can find someone with a cell phone that works," Frank called after me. "If I find one, I'll let you know."

"Sounds good."

"Hey," the guy from the Volvo shouted. "Where the hell do you think you're going?"

I stopped, turned and fought to keep the annoyance out of my voice.

"To help my friend and this woman. Her daughter is missing."

"Bullshit. You're not leaving the scene. You guys rear-ended me. I don't even have your insurance information yet. Just stay put until the cops get here."

"For fuck's sake," I sputtered. "Leave the scene? Take a look around you, dickhead. The entire interstate is one big scene. Where would I go?"

I turned my back on him and walked towards Charlie and the hysterical mother.

"Hey!" Volvo's shout was hoarse and shaky. "Don't you walk away from me. I said get back here, goddamn it."

"Fuck you," I called over my shoulder, and then punctuated it with, "Jackass."

His footsteps pounded across the asphalt. Before I could turn to face him, Charlie was at my side, his fists clenched. Several onlookers watched us warily. A few of them looked excited. Here was something to take their minds off their troubles: fellow commuters getting in a fist fight.

"Get out of my way," Volvo growled.

"Not another step, buddy." Charlie's expression was grim. Anger smoldered in his eyes.

Volvo stopped in his tracks, shaking with rage. "You guys fucking rear-ended me. I've got witnesses."

"Look," I shouted. "I don't know what your malfunction is, but in case you haven't noticed, you're not the only one in trouble here. Seriously. Take a good look around, man. Something's happened. Something is wrong. People are dead—and others are missing. Now, I'm sorry we hit you, but maybe you should have been paying attention to the road instead of talking on your fucking cell phone!"

"You—"

Charlie stepped between us, and drew himself up to his full height. He jabbed a finger at the yuppie's chest. "That woman's baby is missing. We're going to help her find it. When we're done, if you still want to tangle, then I'll be glad to kick your ass. But if you don't back down right now, so help me God, I will fucking kill you."

"You won't do shit."

"Think not?" Charlie smiled. "Try me."

Volvo's fists were clenched so tight that his knuckles had turned white. But he backed off.

"You just want to bang her," he accused Charlie from a safe distance. "Play good Samaritan and then screw her later on tonight."

Charlie blew him a mock kiss. "Actually, you're more my type. What are you doing later on, after they clean up this mess and tow away the cars? Want to have a drink with me?"

Volvo's ears turned deep red, but he walked away. We watched him go as he shuffled towards his car, casting wary glances at us over his shoulder. The sun glinted off his Rolex watch.

"Too bad he's such a dick," Charlie said. "He's kind of cute."

I chuckled. "No accounting for taste."

The young mother crawled through the weeds and trash at the side of the road. "Britney? Baby?"

Charlie and I hurried to her side.

"We've got to find Britney," she sobbed. "Her car seat is empty. Where's my baby?"

"Don't worry," Charlie soothed. "We'll find her."

She tried to speak, but her words dissolved into tears. Her nose was still bleeding.

"Hey, Steve!"

I turned to see Frank running towards us.

"Sit down here," Charlie coaxed the woman, easing her onto the grass. "We'll find your daughter. She's got to be close by."

"Do you think so?"

"Sure." He smiled reassuringly. "With everything that's going on, we weren't properly introduced earlier. What's your name?"

"St-Stephanie." She wiped her bloody nose with the back of her hand.

"Alright, Stephanie. My name's Charlie and this is Steve. We're going to help you look for Britney, okay?"

She sniffed and nodded. Frank came up to us, panting and out of breath.

"You manage to get a hold of anybody?" I asked him.

"Cell phones are all on the fritz now, but I talked to a trucker in that rig over there. Nice guy. He's got a CB that's working. Said there's some weird shit going on."

Several other people converged on our location and began helping search for baby Britney. Stephanie seemed to regain her resolve.

"My husband's missing, too," one woman sobbed, touching Stephanie's hand. "We were on the tour bus over there on the other side of the highway, on our way back from Atlantic City. I was asleep, and when I woke up after the crash, he was gone."

"Maybe he's helping someone else," Charlie suggested.

The woman nodded. "I guess that's possible." She sounded like she was trying to convince herself.

I pulled Frank aside. "What kind of weird shit did the trucker say is happening?"

"People are missing."

I snorted. "Yeah, I know that."

"But it's not just here: it's happening all around Baltimore; hospitals, schools, offices—everywhere. All of the highways look like this, and the drivers or passengers from some of the cars are missing. The beltway is a disaster area. Four planes have already crashed at BWI and they've had a few more

29

Brian Keene

reporting that their pilot or co-pilot vanished in mid-air. A runaway train smashed into another one downtown."

I rubbed my aching head. "Let me guess. The conductor vanished?"

He nodded. "Yep. Same with a passenger ferry down at the Inner Harbor. The pilot vanished and the ferry rammed the pier. And it seems like everybody all over the city heard that trumpet sound, or whatever the hell it was."

"I don't believe it." I shook my head, stunned at how fast the paranoia and rumors had spread. It was the same way on September 11th, when people reported that planes were heading for Baltimore's Trade Center and the Aberdeen army base and Three Mile Island and Peachbottom nuclear power plants just over the border in Pennsylvania, and that the government had forced down a hijacked airliner over Canadian airspace—and of course none of it had turned out to be true. Now it was happening again.

"Listen," Frank said, "I'm just telling you what the trucker told me. You said it yourself, Steve: your friend's missing. And that woman's baby is missing, too. So are a lot of other folks."

I lowered my voice, making sure the others couldn't hear. "Her baby is either trapped in the wreckage or lying along the side of the road. Craig too, for that matter."

Frank stared into my eyes. "Do you really believe that?"

I opened my mouth to reply, and found that I couldn't, because deep down inside the answer was no. No, I didn't really believe that. As impossible as it all seemed, Frank was right. People were missing. Lots of people. All I had to do was listen, and I could hear their loved ones calling out for them, desperately searching through the snarled lanes of traffic.

Again I thought of Terri. There was a lump in my throat. "I need to get home."

Frank nodded. "We all do. Don't think we'll be going anywhere for a while, though. Not until they get a fleet of tow trucks in here and clear away some of these wrecked cars."

I glanced around for Charlie, and found him in a thin

30

stand of trees alongside the highway, looking for Stephanie's baby. I walked towards him, and Frank followed along behind me. Charlie looked up as we approached. His face was covered with sweat, and a mosquito was biting his ear. He didn't seem to notice.

"What's up?" he asked.

Frank pointed at Charlie's feet. "Well, for starters, you're standing in a patch of poison ivy."

Charlie jumped out of the undergrowth, cursing. I reached out and swatted the mosquito away.

"Thanks." He rubbed his ear.

"Listen," I said, "I need to get home. I have to make sure Terri's okay."

"Terri?" He looked surprised. "Why wouldn't she be okay? She wasn't traveling in this. She's safe at home."

"At the very least, she'll be worried. You saw the traffic helicopter earlier. I'm sure this has made the news already. But it's more than that. Frank here overheard some things on a trucker's CB radio."

"What things?"

"Something's going on, Charlie. People have vanished into thin air, just like Craig."

He didn't reply. His Adam's apple bobbed up and down.

"Charlie—"

"I know," he interrupted me. "Just don't want to think about it. This kind of shit doesn't happen in real life."

Another scream interrupted him.

Charlie looked back out to the road. "But it *is* happening, isn't it? People are missing. Gone. Like they've been abducted by aliens or something."

Frank pulled a red bandana from his back pocket, removed his hardhat and mopped his brow.

"Steve," Charlie continued, his voice barely a whisper, "Craig disappeared before we crashed."

"What?"

He sighed. "I didn't tell you before because it sounded crazy. Shit, I didn't believe it myself. Thought maybe I banged my head in the crash or something. Got mixed up. Hallucinated. But that's not what happened. He disappeared

31

in mid-fucking-sentence, dude. I saw it happen. He was there, and then we heard that blast, and he was gone. Then we wrecked, and after that I was confused, and then you woke up and—what the hell is going on?"

I shook my head. "I don't know, man. But right now, I need to get home to Terri. I can't explain it, but I've got a bad feeling. Come with me?"

Charlie, Hector, Craig and I carpooled because we all lived in the same town, Shrewsbury, which was just across the border in Pennsylvania. Charlie was single and rented a tiny efficiency apartment over the hardware store on Main Street. Terri and I owned a house just a few blocks away, and both Hector and Craig had lived on the outskirts of town in the new development that had gone in after the Wal-Mart. The town of Shrewsbury was basically just a bed-and-breakfast for people like us, people who were born and raised in Maryland and worked in Baltimore, but had moved out of the state to get away from the higher taxes.

"Come on," I urged. "Please? Let's go home."

Charlie pointed at the people combing the road for Stephanie's daughter. "But what about her baby?"

"There's nothing we can do." I hated how callous I sounded, but my mind was made up. "Let's face it—they're not going to find anything. Britney is gone."

"They might," he insisted. "She could have been thrown from the car."

"Stephanie's car isn't even damaged," I said. "Her daughter is among the missing. We can't help her. Maybe when the cops get here, they can do something."

"If it's as bad as I think it is," Frank added, "then I imagine the National Guard is probably out in force. Maybe we should wait for them to show up."

"And do what?" I asked. "If it really is that bad, their hands are full. If people are disappearing, if planes and trains are crashing like you say they are, then the National Guard are going to be doing more than clearing traffic jams. There's liable to be riots, looting—all kinds of shit."

Frank wrung his bandana out and shoved it back in his pocket. "Yeah, I guess you're right. Hadn't thought of that."

Another scream rang out, followed by a horn.

"So where do you guys live?" Frank asked, shuffling his feet.

"Shrewsbury," Charlie told him. "Just off Exit One on the Pennsylvania side."

"I'm pretty close to you," Frank said. "Parkton—last exit in Maryland."

"That's where the Park-and-Ride is, right?" Charlie asked.

"Yeah. Listen, you guys care if I tag along with you?"

I shrugged. "Sure. There's safety in numbers."

"Safety?" Charlie cocked his head. "Safe from what?"

Instead of replying, I checked my cell phone. There was still no service, but the clock was working. It was 5:30 p.m.

"Britney!" Stephanie screamed from the tall grass. "Where are you, baby?"

Britney didn't answer.

None of the missing did.

3

Twenty minutes later, after weaving our way through the snarled traffic, we reached Exit 18—Warren Road and Cockeysville. Those were twenty minutes of dazed and hysterical commuters, wrecked vehicles, and mangled, bloody bodies. Twenty minutes of despair and hopelessness that grew with each tortured cry. Twenty minutes of diesel fumes and burning rubber. Twenty minutes that seemed like an eternity.

We stopped to rest and took seats on the guardrail, right beneath the exit sign. Frank breathed heavily, gasping for air, and the veins stood out in his face. He looked like he was ready to have a heart attack. All three of us were drenched with sweat, and Charlie and I both had dark circles under the arms of our dress shirts.

"Whew," Frank panted. "Talk about taking the long way home."

"I'm still not sure we should be doing this," Charlie grumbled.

"Both of us got banged up when Hector hit the construction barrier. Should we be walking this far? I don't know about you, Steve, but my head hurts. What if we've got concussions or something?"

I cracked my neck to get rid of the stiffness. "I don't care. Only thing I want to do now is get home to Terri."

There was a stone quarry to our right, nestled in the shallow valley below. One of the facility's buildings was on fire. Orange flames flickered across the rooftop, and thick, black smoke poured from the doors and windows, drifting up the hill and billowing over the highway. Workers scurried around the building like panicking ants. A few more employees lay on the ground, unmoving. There were no fire trucks or ambulances in sight. We'd only seen one state police cruiser since the Timonium exit, and it was deserted, parked along the side of the road. I'd wondered if the officer disappeared with the rest or had abandoned the vehicle afterward.

My headache grew worse.

"You guys got any aspirin?"

They both shook their heads.

"I'd kill for a beer right now," Frank said.

I wondered about the bars. Would they be jam-packed tonight, filled to overflowing as word of the disaster spread and people's loved ones didn't come home? Would people flock to them, seeking comfort in the presence of others? Or would they all go to church or temple instead? Personally, I'd always thought that there wasn't much difference between a tavern and a place of worship.

Frank watched the flames spread in the quarry. A second building caught fire.

"Where are the authorities?" he asked. "Why aren't they doing something? That whole place is gonna be toast. And it looks like they've got injured."

Charlie took off his shoe and shook a stone out. "Busy elsewhere, I guess."

"They can't all be elsewhere," Frank said. "Some of them should have responded to the fire by now. At least an ambulance."

"Maybe they can't get through," I said.

Charlie frowned. "Like we said earlier, maybe they're shorthanded. Or some of them might have disappeared, too."

I considered this. There was no rhyme or reason to the missing people, nothing to indicate why they'd been taken. From what we'd seen, it affected all races, genders and age groups. The only thing I'd noticed was that we hadn't seen a single infant. Just lots of empty car seats. Were all of the babies missing? I wondered if this could be the glorious Rapture that Terri and her parents had talked about, but decided against it. I'd seen several priests, nuns and preachers among the survivors, and a dozen occupied vehicles with

35

Jesus bumper stickers and license plates. Plenty of Christians were left behind. And Craig was a Christian too, and hadn't necessarily believed in the Rapture, yet he was missing along with the rest. The only common denominator was that everybody had vanished at the same time, immediately after that bizarre blast—except for the black guy, Gabriel. He'd vanished later, after helping me. He'd told me something, just before he disappeared. I tried to remember what it was but the words wouldn't come. Trying to figure it out made my head hurt, so I stopped.

"Maybe it really was a terrorist attack," Charlie said. "Maybe they got their hands on some kind of black ops weapon."

"It isn't that," Frank replied.

"How do you know?"

Frank shrugged. "I don't. I'd just rather not think about the possibility, is all."

"So what is it then?"

"It just is what it is."

A disheveled man wandered towards us. He reeked, the stench reminding me of a litter box. The crotch of his trousers had a wet splotch where he'd pissed himself. There was a long, bloody gash on his forehead.

"Excuse me." His eyes looked dazed. "Do you guys have the time?"

I checked my cell phone. "Almost six."

"Thanks. How about a cigarette? Got one of those?"

All three of us shook our heads.

The man lowered his voice to a conspiratorial whisper. "Need a smoke. I keep thinking that maybe I should find an unguarded gas station and steal some cigarettes. But I've never done anything like that before."

"I wouldn't try it," Charlie said. "The police are probably out by now, patrolling for that kind of thing. I'm sure things will be back to normal by tomorrow."

"Normal?" The man blinked at him. "I guess you guys haven't heard."

I looked up, holding my breath to avoid breathing in his stink. "Heard what?"

"Alien abduction," he gasped. "Everybody's talking about it. All these folks that are missing? They were abducted by aliens. You know—the Grays, like you see on TV? The ones they talk about late at night on the radio? We're under attack!"

"Get the fuck outta here." Frank spat on the pavement. "Little gray men, my ass."

"I'm serious," the man insisted. "This is happening all over the world, not just here. New York, Washington, London, Moscow, Budapest, Jerusalem—you name it. I heard they even got the President and some of his cabinet. Disappeared right out of the White House. That's why he hasn't addressed the nation. Famous people, too. You guys know that rapper, Prosper Johnson?"

Frank shook his head. Charlie and I nodded. Terri and I had seen him in concert the first year we were dating, back when we still did fun things like that (these days, as we got a little older, we were happy to stay home and play a game of *Uno*).

"Well," the man continued, "you know how he was up for the Nobel Peace Prize, on account of stopping the violence in L.A., right? He was giving a speech on TV. All the cable news stations were carrying it. He vanished live, on camera."

"Seriously?" Charlie asked.

The man raised his right hand. "Swear to God. Disappeared in mid fucking sentence. Fucking aliens beamed him up or something, just like everybody else. People are going nuts. Everything's in chaos."

"Alien abduction," Charlie said. "You really believe that?"

"You got a better explanation?"

None of us did, and the man stumbled away. We watched him stop and bum a cigarette off another man, and tell him the same story.

"So," Charlie said. "Prosper Johnson is among the missing. That's too bad."

"I hate that rap shit," Frank muttered. "Bunch a black guys singing about how much money they got, and how many bitches they got and this gun and that gun."

Charlie threw a pebble over the guardrail. "It's not just 'black guys.' There are plenty of white rappers."

"What's your point?"

"Well, no offense, Frank, but that's kind of a racist statement."

Frank scowled. "How is that racist?"

"You're implying that all black people rap. That's like saying all Asians are good at math, or that all gay men watch *Will and Grace*. It's a stereotype. I'm gay, and I hate that fucking show."

"I ain't a racist."

"You work in construction, right?"

Frank nodded.

"You mean to tell me you and your buddies never stood around on the site and told jokes about queers?"

"Don't start with that politically-correct bullshit. Talk about stereotypes—you think all construction workers stand around and make fun of gay people and whistle at women? You think we're all just a bunch of ignorant, uneducated rednecks?"

Charlie opened his mouth to respond, but Frank cut him off and continued.

"You ever tell a Polack joke?"

Charlie shrugged, then reluctantly nodded.

"So I could call you a racist, too, then. You're making a joke—a stereotype—about how stupid my ancestors are supposed to be. Well, I ain't stupid and I ain't a racist. All I did was state a fact. Most rappers are black. That's where it started, right?"

Charlie turned to me and changed the subject. "How far is it to Shrewsbury, you think?"

I took my tie off and wrapped it around my head for a sweatband. "About thirty more miles."

"And how far have we gone?"

"One mile."

"Shit." He stood up. "At this rate, it'll be morning before we get home. We'd better keep moving."

I tried calling Terri again, but there was still no service, not even when we passed directly beneath a cell phone tower.

We stayed on the side of the road, trying to keep a steady

pace. The tension eased between Charlie and Frank. We made small talk. Frank talked about his job, and we told him about ours. Then we came to a bridge. The guardrail forced us into traffic, and we walked between the cars. People leaned back in their seats with the windows rolled down, or lounged on the hoods. Some asked for news, or for help finding a companion, but we had time for neither.

As we passed the Shawan Road exit, I looked to my right at the shopping center, light rail station, hotel and convention center. People milled about in the parking lots. Cars moved on the streets, albeit slowly. The traffic lights at the bottom of the exit ramp still worked and, for the most part, drivers obeyed them. On the surface, things looked surprisingly normal, but I knew it was an illusion. I wondered how many people had vanished in the darkness of the movie theatre, or from the swimming pool at the hotel, or sitting on the train. Did their loved ones even know they were missing yet? Did they expect them to come home tonight?

Footsteps thudded on the macadam ahead of us. We looked up as a guy in a charcoal-colored business suit ran past us, shouting at the top of his lungs to nobody in particular that the stock market had crashed. His tie fluttered behind him as he dashed by. He skidded in the gravel, almost losing his balance. Then, without even glancing at Frank, Charlie or myself, he vaulted over the guardrail and slid down the embankment. A cloud of dust marked his passage.

We passed by a Cadillac with its driver's door hanging open. The keys dangled from the ignition, and were turned to the accessory option. The radio was on, tuned to the news, and sure enough, the stock market had crashed, just like the man had been shouting. I wondered if this was his car. A cell phone lay on the passenger seat. The floor was littered with fast food bags and Styrofoam coffee cups.

"Should we take the car?" Charlie asked.

I stared at him in disbelief. "This isn't fucking Thunderdome, man. Stealing cars is still against the law."

"Well it ain't like whoever left it here needs it. Maybe the driver vanished."

"That's not the point."

39

Charlie glanced up the highway. "We've got a long walk home, Steve. We'd be there in an hour with the Caddy."

"No." Frank stepped forward. "Much as I hate to say it—believe me, my feet hurt already—but a car will just slow us down. Look how congested things are. Traffic's not moving."

We listened to the frantic reporter for a minute. The news was bad, getting worse by the second, and the reporter's voice kept breaking. The world's financial markets were in an uproar. Millions were reported missing, including politicians, C.E.O.'s, world leaders, religious figures and celebrities. They'd vanished from their homes, their cars and their places of business. According to NASA, a Russian cosmonaut had even gone missing off the International Space Station, leaving one countryman and an American astronaut behind. Planes fell from the sky. Trains crashed. The highways were deathtraps. A nuclear reactor at a power plant in China was reportedly in meltdown. Fires and rioting had broken out in just about every major city on Earth, and there were dozens of reports of authorities shooting looters and declaring martial law amidst the unrest. Religious fighting swept through Asia and the Middle East, with the worst of it centered in Israel. All of this within a few hours. I wondered how much worse things would get before it was over.

Charlie gave one last, lingering look at the Cadillac, and then we continued on, trying to ignore the screams and plaintive calls for loved ones from those left behind. I saw surreal signs of the missing as well: an abandoned baby doll in the middle lane, an empty wheelchair, a pair of empty shoes, a castaway purse, and a cluster of roadside construction vehicles—steamroller, bulldozer, and dump trucks. Judging by the path of destruction, it looked like the steamroller had kept going after its operator disappeared, flattening orange traffic cones and toolboxes.

A few minutes later, we came across a tractor-trailer. The seal on the back door had been broken and a gang of youths was looting it, hauling away televisions and DVD players. Most of the teens were armed. Stranded motorists minded their own business, pretending they didn't see it happening. Charlie, Frank and I did the same. There were no cops around. Not even the distant sound of sirens. The last thing we needed right now was more trouble, and besides, stopping would just slow us down even more and impede me getting home to Terri. So they were stealing electronics. It wasn't our problem. It was somebody else's.

The construction ended after Shawan Road and the lanes expanded again, making it easier for us to navigate. Traffic was less snarled here, and although there were still plenty of wrecked cars with missing, injured, or dead occupants, many more had driven on. Several passed slowly by us, and Frank choked on the exhaust fumes.

"Maybe it's clearing up," Charlie said.

I nodded, doubtful.

Charlie grabbed my arm. "Let's go back and get the Caddy. There's no sense walking anymore. Traffic's moving."

"We're not stealing a car," I said. "That would make us no better than those kids ripping off that home electronics rig."

The driver of an ice delivery van was handing out his melting inventory for free to passersby. We stopped and got a bag, and sucked on ice cubes as we walked. It started to get dark about 6:30 p.m., and though the sun was still clinging to the horizon, the air grew chilly. More cars passed us, but nobody offered a ride. We saw other people walking, too.

"Maybe we should have waited with our vehicles after all," Frank said. "Charlie's right. Looks like things are starting to move again."

I shook my head. "It'll be hours—maybe even morning— before they get this mess sorted out. They're moving, but I bet it gets blocked up again around the turn. I'm going on. If we can hitch a ride later on, then that's all the better, but I'm not stealing a car."

Down in the valley, on the north side of the highway, a church burned. It looked deserted.

Charlie asked, "I wonder if Stephanie ever found Britney?"

"I doubt it," Frank said. "I think there's a lot of people who aren't coming home tonight."

"Maybe not," I said, "but I am."

Charlie and Frank stopped, and looked back the way we'd come.

I thought about Terri, and how we'd parted that morning. It wasn't bad, not at all. No fighting or arguing or anything. It just wasn't—special. The same daily routine we'd both grown used to. The alarm went off at five. I got up. She hit snooze. I took a shower while she hit snooze two more times. Then I tickled her to get her moving. While she showered, I made a pot of coffee—always something good, Columbian or Kenyan, usually. We'd never been big breakfast eaters, so we sat in the living room and watched the news and drank our coffee. We didn't say much. We never did. Neither one of us were what you'd call morning people, and conversation wasn't first on our list until the caffeine kicked in. Then Hector pulled up out front and honked the horn. I gave Terri a quick kiss on the lips, and told her I loved her, and hurried for the door. She'd told me she loved me and that it was my turn to cook dinner when I got home, and then shut the door behind me. In a few minutes she'd start work as well. Luckily for Terri, she worked from our home.

Typical suburban morning, and I'd gotten the chance to tell her I loved her. But I hadn't really said it. I'd mouthed the words, and I'd meant them, of course, but that's all they were—perfunctory words, just like the kiss and the coffee and the snooze button on the alarm clock. They were ritual. I needed to tell her from my heart, to say more than just "I love you." I needed to hold her in my arms and make sure she understood me; that she knew I really meant it, and wasn't just going through the motions. Needed her to know I was okay.

Needed to know that she was okay.

"Steve?" Charlie interrupted my thoughts. "What about Hector's body? Are we doing the right thing, leaving him behind like that?"

I turned. "Look, if you guys want to go back, I understand. But I've got to get home to Terri."

I kept walking. After a moment, they followed me.

4

We reached the overpass for Thornton Mill Road by 8:00 p.m., and that was when things started to get worse. The interstate crossed over Western Run Creek. Darkness had fallen by then, throwing everything into shadow. As we tromped over the bridge, I heard the creek trickling below us, but couldn't see it. The sound was eerie. Ghostly, as if the creek had vanished too and its spirit was haunting this place. Traffic was blocked again. A tanker truck lay on its side in front of the overpass. Those with four-wheel drive vehicles and motorcycles went around it, driving up over the embankment and onto the road above. Others parked their cars and milled about, exchanging gossip and small talk. I noticed that nobody was getting too close to the wrecked tanker, and when I saw the HazMat markings on its side, and the dark stains where liquid had spilled out onto the road, I understood why.

Away from the wreckage, someone had started a bonfire in a rusty fifty-five gallon drum and several people were gathered around it, warming themselves by the fire. Many of them stared upward, and when we got closer, we did the same.

A man hung from the overpass, the rope around his neck twisting slowly in the night breeze. A piece of cardboard had been stapled to his chest, the words 'CHILD MOLESTER' scrawled on it with black magic marker in big block letters. His face looked strange in the flickering firelight. Weird shadows danced across his skin. His bowels had let go, and shit had rolled down his legs and splattered onto the pavement beneath him. The crowd kept its distance from this, too.

43

Charlie made a noise like someone had punched him in the stomach. He turned his head and threw up all over the road.

Frank said, "What the fuck happened here?"

Cautiously, we approached the group gathered around the fire. They eyed us suspiciously. One of them, an older Hispanic man with a silver beard, nodded.

"How you doing?"

"As good as can be expected," Frank said. "We walked from Timonium. You folks care if we rest here for a minute?"

"Help yourself."

The man moved aside, and the others followed his lead, making room for us. They seemed to relax a bit. They were a weird assortment, business suits and blue jeans, silk and denim, gold jewelry and dirty flannel.

"I'm Tony," the guy with the silver beard said. "Was on my way to work when it happened. Guess I'll have to use a sick day. I work nights at the McCormick plant."

I introduced Charlie, Frank and myself. Nods were exchanged, but nobody shook hands or traded business cards.

Tony studied us. "You guys walked all the way from Timonium?"

"Yeah." I nodded. "Traffic's at a standstill down there."

"It's not moving too quickly here, either," a middle-aged black woman noted. "Not with that overturned truck blocking the road."

"Yeah," Frank said, "but at least it's still moving here. The four-wheel drives and the motorcycles are getting through. Down there, the only thing moving is the wind."

"Lots of accidents?" Tony asked.

I warmed my hands over the open flames. "Yeah, a bunch of wrecks and lots of people hurt or dead. How about here?"

"Here, too. Lots of dead—and even more missing."

"Do they know what caused it?" Frank rubbed the back of his neck.

"So far, we've heard everything from terrorists to aliens. Somebody even said it was some kind of hallucinogen, sprayed through the air by a crop duster or something. Chemtrails, the guy said. I don't know about that, though."

Tony looked up at the moon. I noticed his eyes avoided the hanging man.

"There's all kinds of rumors and speculation," he said, "but no real news. We had our car radios on for a while, but none of us wanted to kill our batteries or run out of gas. Last we heard, nobody knew the cause. Only thing we know for sure is that everybody heard that trumpet noise."

"Us, too," I confirmed.

The black woman laughed, but there was no humor in it. "They heard it around the world. Toronto, Los Angeles, Paris, Beijing—and soon as it happened, millions of people vanished in an instant."

Frank stepped back from the fire and mopped his brow. "What's the government doing about it?"

Tony snorted. "Right now? Nothing."

"But they've got to do something," Frank said. "The Department of Homeland Security and F.E.M.A.—that's what they're for. At the very least, they should mobilize the National Guard. What the hell's the President doing? Hiding on Air Force One again while everything turns to shit?"

"No," Tony whispered. "The President's among the missing."

I shook my head. The guy we'd encountered earlier, the one who'd pissed himself, had been right after all. I wondered if he'd been right about the gray aliens part, too.

Conversation died after that. One man produced a bottle of diet soda, and another had a whiskey flask. Both were passed around, along with cigarettes. The group drank and smoked in silence.

Finally, Charlie broke the quiet. "So, anybody want to tell us what happened to the guy hanging from the noose?"

The group shifted uneasily. Charlie pointed but none of them would look directly at the swinging corpse. Nobody answered him, so Charlie tried again.

"He's like the proverbial elephant in the corner, isn't he? Aren't any of you going to tell us what happened?"

They glanced at one another.

"Skinheads," Tony said. "A gang of skinheads; six of them. There was a little girl. Both her parents were missing.

That guy—" he cocked a thumb at the swinging dead man, "tried to coax her inside his car. A lot of us saw it, and it was clear that the girl didn't know him. She started yelling and ran away. So we all confronted him. He denied it at first, but the girl swore she didn't know him, and that he'd shown her his 'wee wee.' That was all it took. Before we could do anything about it, the skinheads jumped him."

The black woman pulled her hands back from the fire. "Beat the hell out of him is what they did."

"Yeah," Tony agreed. "They did that, too. Then they put that sign on him and strung him up. After that, they torched his car." He pointed to the far lane and, sure enough, there was a burned out steel shell sitting on four heat-warped tires.

Charlie shuddered. "And you people just let them?"

"Hey," Tony said, "there were seven of them."

"I thought you said there were six?"

"Six. Seven. What's the difference? They all had guns. A few of us tried calling the cops, but our cell phones aren't working. And besides…"

"What?"

Tony shrugged. "The guy deserved it. I mean, think about what he did. He was going to kidnap and rape a little girl who'd lost her parents. He'd have probably killed her after he was done. You see it every day on the news."

Charlie looked around. "Where's the little girl? Is she okay?"

The black woman pointed. "She's asleep in the back of that van over there. She's safe. We're watching over her, until . . ."

"Until what?"

She stared Charlie in the eyes. "Until things get back to normal. Until someone comes along and tells us what to do."

Frank took a sip of whiskey as it passed by him. He closed his eyes and a look of sheer bliss crossed his face.

"Besides," Tony said, "better him than us, right? They were skinheads. They could just have easily turned on us."

"That's right," the black woman agreed.

"So where are these skinheads now?" I asked.

The black woman pointed up the highway. "They moved

on when it was over. Good riddance, if you ask me."

"Guess they didn't want to hang around." Tony smiled at his own gallows humor.

"I don't believe this shit," Charlie said. "Skinheads, my ass."

Tony's smile turned to a frown. "What? Are you calling me a liar?"

I took Charlie by the arm. "Come on. Let it alone."

"Fuck that! They—"

"I mean it, Charlie." I squeezed his arm hard, insisting. "Let's go."

"But—"

I thanked the group gathered around the fire. "Appreciate your help. We need to get moving."

They nodded in understanding, but several of them, Tony and the black woman included, glared at Charlie. He let me lead him away. A moment later, Frank followed us.

"Where you guys heading, anyway?" Tony called out.

"Pennsylvania," I said, without looking back.

"What's in Pennsylvania?"

"My wife."

"What else?"

"That's what we intend to find out."

Frank, Charlie and I continued on side by side, and when we passed under the body, and heard the rope creaking, none of us glanced upward.

There was no time to hang around, after all.

5

We didn't talk for a long time as all of us were out of breath. My thoughts were on Terri. Random images, really. When we met in college. Our first date. First argument. First time we made love. Our wedding day, and when we moved into the house. I missed her.

Frank finally broke the silence. "Anybody know a good joke?"

"How's this?" Charlie said. "A Jew, a Polack, and a homo are walking down the middle of the interstate at night . . ."

Frank and I both grinned.

"What's the punch-line?" I asked.

Charlie shrugged. "I don't know. Guess we'll find out soon enough."

Half a mile later, we came across the Soapbox Man, as Charlie called him. Wild-eyed and frothing, his clothes and hair in disarray, he'd climbed atop the hood of an abandoned car and was preaching the Gospel to all who would listen. Surprisingly, he'd attracted a small crowd. They passed a bottle of wine around and listened, staring at him with rapt attention, their eyes shining in the darkness, their mouths glistening wet.

"It's the end times," he hissed. "The angel has played the trump and the seven seals will be opened! Blood. Fire. Disease. And another angel will appear, the angel of death, and he shall ride a pale horse."

We crept past, trying to avoid making eye contact with the crazed preacher.

"This is your fault," the man roared, jabbing a finger at the crowd. "You have brought this upon yourselves, because you had ears but did not hear. You had eyes but did not see.

You denied God, and put other gods before Him. Now He has called His faithful home, and has left me behind to warn you of what will come. You removed Him from your schools and courtrooms and allowed sodomites to marry and babies to be killed in their wombs. Now you will pay the price for your sins. This is the start of the long, dark night."

"Fucking nutcase," Frank grumbled. "As if things weren't bad enough."

After we'd safely made it past the group and were out of earshot, we picked up our pace again.

"Think that's true?" Charlie asked.

Frank snorted. "What? That God took everybody away because of abortion and gay marriage?"

"Well . . . yeah."

"Fucking bullshit," Frank said. "I've got an easier time believing in little gray men, and I don't believe that either."

I grinned. "I take it you're not religious?"

Frank scowled. "Used to be, until my wife left. Came home from work one day and she'd cleaned the house out. Left me a dinner plate, fork and spoon. And the lawnmower. Come to find out she'd been cheating on me for the last six months. Ended up moving in with the guy, and left me holding the mortgage. We got divorced. I filed for bankruptcy while she got remarried."

Charlie whistled. "Damn. That sucks, man."

"Yeah, it does. After that, I just quit believing. Seemed easier that way. I mean, you take a look around and all you see are wars and famine and people dying of cancer and little kids getting snatched by sick fucks like the guy back at the bridge. There's just too much heartache and pain. Where's the love? God's supposed to be love, right? I don't think He exists. Think we're all walking around trying to live our lives according to a book that was pieced together when dinosaurs still roamed the earth."

"So you're an atheist?" I asked.

"Yep," Frank said. "And probably going straight to Hell for it. Heh—I don't believe in God but I still believe in Hell. Ain't that funny?"

Charlie and I agreed that it was.

"How about you guys?" Frank asked. "You atheists?"

"I'm agnostic, I guess," Charlie answered. "I believe in something. I just don't know what. Certainly not the Christian God. His believers say that He hates me. I've heard that all my life. Supposedly, He nuked an entire city just because of people like me. So fuck that—I ain't following. But I do think there's something out there. Something that maybe we're not meant to understand. I believe in ghosts and stuff like that, so I guess that's proof of an afterlife."

Frank nodded. "But not a Heaven?"

"No," Charlie said. "At least, not the way you mean. No clouds and people with wings on their backs, flying around and playing the harp. If you want to see that, there's a gay bar in York I can take you to."

Frank started laughing and Charlie joined him. They both stopped, clutching their bellies and slapping each other on the shoulder. Despite my eagerness to get home, I was glad for the break, and even happier to see that the tension between the two was easing. When they'd gotten their breath back, we started down the road again.

"How about you, Steve?" Frank asked. "What do you believe?"

"I don't know. I was born and raised Jewish. My wife and her parents are born-again Christians. I don't know what that makes me. I guess I don't really believe in anything, other than that I wish everybody could get along."

Charlie nodded. "I can't remember who said it, but there's a quote that goes, 'There's enough religion in the world to make people hate one another, but not enough to make them love one another.'"

"I agree with that," Frank said.

We walked on in silence. A group of crows were gathered along the side of the road, picking at a corpse. In the darkness, I couldn't tell if it was a man or a woman, or what had killed it. Stranded motorists ignored the birds. One of the scavengers took flight with something pink hanging from its beak.

A murder, I thought. *A group of crows is called a murder.*

"But what if they're right?" Charlie asked again. "The

Soapbox Man and his crowd. What if this really was the Rapture or the Second Coming or whatever they call it?"

Frank shrugged. "If that's true, then God called everybody home and we don't get to go."

"Sure we do," I said. "We're walking home right now."

"Yeah," Frank replied. "But to get to the home they're talking about, we'd have an awful long way to walk."

I sighed. "Seems to me like we have a long walk ahead of us either way."

"Yeah," Frank agreed. "Wish we'd have brought along some of that whiskey those people back at the fire gave us."

"I've got a new joke," Charlie said. "A Jew, a Polack, and a homo are walking to Heaven, pissed off that God left them behind . . ."

"What's the punch line?" Frank asked.

"I don't know." Charlie smiled. "Like I said earlier, we'll just have to wait and see."

Charlie's words ran through my mind. Home. Heaven. They were pretty much the same thing, as far as I was concerned. Christians said that when they died, they went home to be with the Lord. They called Heaven home. My heaven was home, too—at home with my wife. I'd walk all night to be with her again, if I had to. And if God really had called His children home and took them all to Heaven, then I'd walk there to find her, too.

In either case, it was a long way to walk.

6

We reached Exit 24—Butler and Sparks—around 8:40 p.m. The suburbs and industrial parks had given way to woodlands and farms. Lots of cars traveled past us now, both on-road and off. Those with four-wheel drive raced through the fields and pastures, short-cutting around the slow-moving traffic. Some without four-wheel drive tried it too, and wound up stuck in the mud. We had to raise our voices over the spinning tires and blaring horns as they splattered each other's windshields with mud.

We stuck close to the guardrail as the traffic passed. Frank and Charlie looked as tired as I felt. The cold air raised gooseflesh on my sweaty skin. The muscles in my legs ached and my feet had blisters on them. When I stumbled, Charlie caught me.

"We should rest again," he suggested.

I shook my head. "Can't. Need to get home to Terri."

"You sound like a broken record, dude. You're not going to do Terri any good if you end up lying alongside the highway, dying from exhaustion."

"He's right," Frank panted. "I ain't as young as you guys. I need another break."

Reluctantly, I allowed Charlie to guide me over to the guardrail. We sat down on it. Another vehicle passed by. The woman behind the wheel looked shell-shocked. She stared straight ahead, her eyes not seeing.

A big guy in a mud-splattered, olive-colored trench coat approached us. He didn't seem wary or afraid. His head was shaved, but long, wispy sideburns framed his leering face. The right lens in his glasses was cracked in a spider-web pattern. He smelled like booze.

52

"Hi." He smiled. "My name's Carlton. What's yours?"

I returned his smile, still unsure of his motives.

"I'm Steve. This is Charlie and Frank."

"Nice to meet you." His voice was softer than I'd expected, given his size.

"I take it you got stranded, too?"

He ignored my question. "The mall is menstruating."

"What?"

More cars filed past us.

"The mall, down in Hunt Valley? It's menstruating. A great ocean floods forth."

"Uh, you mean…bleeding?"

Carlton nodded vigorously. "Really. It is. Just like in the Bible. 'And behold, the malls shall menstruate.' The Book of Meat, chapter twelve; verse two."

Frank groaned under his breath. Carlton didn't seem to notice.

"There's cheese in his head," our new friend continued. "Fishy-fleshed cheese, just like they said there'd be."

"That's nice," I said, giving Frank and Charlie a nervous glance.

First it was the Soapbox Man, shouting and preaching from the hood of his car. Now this. I wondered just how many people had gone insane in the immediate aftermath of the disappearances.

"Are you folks going home?" Carlton asked, smoothing the wrinkles from his trench coat.

Charlie and Frank remained speechless, and I hesitated. Clearly, the guy was drunk or insane—or both. The last thing I wanted was a crazy person following us home. But before I could distract him, Frank spoke up.

"Yeah, we're just trying to get home. Gotta be moving on now, actually."

Carlton glanced down the highway, staring into the darkness. Then he looked back at us and smiled. His eyes seemed to twinkle.

"You can't go home. The others went home. He called them home. But not us. We've been left behind."

I shivered in the darkness. Beside me, I felt Charlie do

the same. Could it be a coincidence that we'd just had this conversation, or was something else at work?

Frank cleared his throat. "It was nice talking to you, Carlton."

Carlton shuffled away from us, then turned around. "This is level six, if you come through the Labyrinth. Level six. Soon, if we stay here, we'll all have to wear the mark. If we want to buy anything, we'll have to wear it. The number is six one six. That's the number of the Beast. We'll wear it, and then we'll get really painful sores, and the seas will turn to blood, just like the mall did."

None of us responded. What do you say to something like that?

"I'm getting out," Carlton said. "I know a doorway."

He walked on, and we watched him go. He stopped farther up the road and talked to a group of migrant workers sitting in the back of a stalled pick-up truck. As we listened to their conversation, it became clear to us that none of the men spoke English, but that was okay, because we weren't sure that Carlton did either.

Another helicopter hovered overhead, low enough to stir up roadside litter and other debris. Hamburger wrappers, cigarette butts, newspapers and plastic cups swirled in a funnel cloud. People on the ground waved their arms and shouted for help, but the chopper flew on. The crowd cursed the pilot.

Charlie took a deep breath and exhaled. "I've been thinking."

"What about?" I turned to him.

"That guy back there at the Thornton Mill Road overpass."

"Tony? The one at the fire?"

"Yeah, him. I think he was lying about the skinheads. I mean, I've got no love for skinheads, don't get me wrong. But it seems like anytime we need a cultural boogeyman in this country, we lay it on a group like that. Skinheads. Muslim terrorists. Satanic daycare instructors. Republicans."

"What's your point?" Frank asked.

"What if it wasn't skinheads that hanged that guy? What

if it was Tony and the other people that were there?"

I rubbed my tired eyes. "Come on, Charlie. You saw them. Most of that group were business people, just like us. Regular people. They're not going to resort to vigilante justice."

"Why not? Things have gotten real weird real quick. The mob rules, man. People have vanished, authorities aren't around, the survivors are scared, and nobody knows what's going on. Sounds like a recipe for disaster to me."

A black Labrador scampered by, its nose to the ground. When Charlie called out to it, the dog ran away, tail tucked between its legs. It must have belonged to somebody because it had a bright red collar around its neck, complete with dog tags. Whimpering, it disappeared.

"I'm starting to think it's true." Frank scratched the back of his neck.

"What?" Charlie asked. "That regular, everyday people hung that guy?"

"No. That aliens abducted everybody. It sounds silly, but could that actually happen?"

"There's no such things as aliens," I said. "It's just another bullshit rumor. They don't exist."

Frank gazed up at the stars. "Just like God..."

"So what's your theory, Steve?" Charlie asked. "We've seen a lot more since it first happened. Where do you think Craig and all these other people went?"

We watched as a Lexus, its speakers rattling with a thudding bass line, swerved to avoid a pedestrian. The driver blew his horn. The man in the road shook his fist and shouted curses.

"I don't know," I admitted, after the car had passed. "But it's not fucking aliens and it's not the Rapture. There has to be a reasonable explanation for what's happened."

"Maybe the scientists did something," Frank said.

"Which scientists?" Charlie asked.

Frank shrugged. "I don't know. Any of them. Maybe there was some kind of accident."

I considered the possibility—a malfunction while experimenting with stealth technology or particle acceleration or teleportation. There was supposed to be a government laboratory somewhere in Hellertown, Pennsylvania that fooled with stuff like that, but those options didn't seem any more plausible than an invisible alien fleet abducting everybody. Not to me, at least.

We shielded our eyes against another pair of approaching headlights—the car was hugging the shoulder, rather than creeping along with the rest of the traffic. The car's horn blared, loud and insistent. All three of us jumped up from our seat, and I almost fell over the guardrail and down the embankment. The horn grew deafening.

"Look out!" Frank shouted.

A black Volvo bore down on us, tires crunching in the gravel along the side of the road. It swerved away at the last second, weaving back into traffic.

Charlie gasped. "That motherfucker . . ."

Our friend, the yuppie from earlier in the day, rolled down his passenger-side window and flipped us his middle finger as he rolled past.

"Hey," he laughed. "Your friend's still back there in Timonium with a pipe through his head!"

"It's him," Charlie shouted, pointing. "The guy from the crash. The one that wanted to sue us!"

"You guys need a ride?"

The Volvo inched forward, moving farther away from us.

I swallowed. "Are you serious?"

"No." The yuppie laughed. "Fuck you."

Then he swerved back onto the shoulder and raced up the highway, scattering other pedestrians out of his way. People hollered at him, but he kept going.

"He needs his ass kicked," Frank sputtered. "Son of a bitch, driving up on us like that. He could have killed somebody."

Both Frank and Charlie shook their middle fingers at the receding taillights. Then the Volvo vanished into the darkness.

"Nothing we can do about it now." I started walking again. "Let's move on."

Groaning with exaggerated effort, Charlie trailed along

after me. Frank stood still, staring back the way we'd come. I followed his gaze. The horizon was on fire. The city of Baltimore's after-dark neon shimmer had been replaced with a hazy, red glow. Smoke curled into the night sky, blacker than the darkness around it.

"My God," I whispered. "What is it?"

"The city's on fire," Frank said. "The whole thing."

"Shit."

"Yeah."

Charlie cleared his throat. "I guess that answers our questions about how busy the authorities are."

We stared in disbelief, watching the glow expand. Baltimore was burning, the entire city engulfed in flames. I wondered if the astronauts on the space station could see it, and if so, what else they were witnessing down here on Earth. The ones who were still onboard the space station, that was. I thought of the news report we'd heard earlier. NASA had claimed that one of them had vanished.

In the woods beyond the exit ramp, something screamed. Human or animal—I couldn't tell which, but the sound was like nails on a chalkboard. I fought to keep from screaming myself, and whispered Terri's name.

"Let's get out of here," I said.

We walked on. A blister broke on the bottom of my heel, and I felt my sock grow wet. I winced, trying to ignore the pain.

"You okay?" Charlie asked, concerned.

I nodded. "Blister. I'll be fine."

"I've said it before," Frank panted, "and I'll say it again: I'd kill for a cold beer right about now. Boy, would that taste good."

"I'd settle for a cell phone that worked," I said.

"I'd like an airplane," Charlie quipped. "Or even a taxi. My feet hurt."

"Mine, too," Frank agreed. "Haven't walked this much since I was in the Army."

"What'd you do in the Army?" I asked, trying to get my thoughts off Terri.

"Construction," he grunted. "Story of my life. I did four

years and then got out. Wish I'd stayed in, though. Could have retired with a full pension at forty. Shit, there wasn't anything going on at the time. Vietnam was over, and Desert Storm was a decade away. But I was stupid, I guess. The old lady wanted to get married, so I got out. Kick myself in the ass for it now, especially after we got divorced. But I was a stupid kid."

"We were all stupid kids once," I said.

"Yeah, and if we only knew then what we know now, right? If I'd re-upped and taken that early retirement, I could've been at home today, instead of walking down this fucking highway in the dark and listening to crazy people talk about God and aliens and bleeding shopping malls."

Charlie and I both laughed, and Frank continued.

"Don't know why I'm so damn eager to get home, anyway. It's not like there's a beautiful woman waiting on me. You're lucky there, Steve."

"I know it," I said. "That's what's keeping my feet moving right now."

"So you live alone?" Charlie asked Frank. "No kids or anything?"

He shook his head sadly. "Nope. Not even a dog. I had some fish, but the little fuckers kept dying on me. I'd buy one, put him in the tank, and a week later he's floating upside down. My ex and I got divorced before we could have any kids. I don't know. It never bothered me much, but the older I get—I would have liked to have a son."

"You still can. You're not that old."

Before Frank could reply, a deer ran across the highway and leaped over the guardrail. We stumbled to a halt, and Charlie gave a surprised little yelp. The doe dashed away across the field, her white tail flashing in the moonlight, before disappearing into a line of trees.

"My heart's racing," Charlie gasped. "Fucking thing scared the shit out of me."

A thought occurred to me. "I wonder if any animals have vanished, too."

Frank and Charlie stared at me as if I were as crazy as Carlton and the Soapbox Man.

"Whatever it is that's happened," I said, "why should it just be limited to us humans? Doesn't make sense."

"We saw that dog a few minutes ago," Frank reminded me. "And there's been plenty of dead animals alongside the road."

"Not road kill. I'm serious. Maybe some of the animals have disappeared. Maybe there's empty kennels and cages at the zoo right now."

Charlie shrugged. "It's something to consider, I guess."

We'd walked another two miles before we heard the voices. As we pressed on through the darkness, they grew louder. There was a large group of people ahead, judging by the sound. We rounded a curve and saw taillights in the distance. Traffic had stopped again, and I wondered what was causing the backup this time. As we got closer, we saw that at least a hundred people stood in the road. Then we smelled something burning: an acrid stench that made my eyes water.

Volvo's car lay on its roof in the middle of the highway, stretched across the median strip and one northbound lane. It was on fire. Smoke poured from the interior, and we heard a high-pitched whining sound. It took me a moment to realize what it was.

Screaming. From inside the car.

Volvo screaming.

A hand flailed from the driver's-side window. The bubbling flesh sloughed off as it waved desperately, but I recognized the expensive Rolex around the charred wrist. The wind picked up, and I smelled roasting meat.

"Jesus . . ." Coughing, I turned away. He may have been a yuppie asshole, but he hadn't deserved this.

A trucker with a small fire extinguisher sprayed foam all over the blackened frame, but it was too late.

Charlie bent over and puked on his shoes. As much as he'd thrown up today, I was amazed that he had anything left inside him. Then I ran to the side of the road and did the same.

Three more cars had been involved in the accident. One was smashed into the guardrail, blocking the other northbound lane. The second was on its side in the southbound lane. The third was spread out all over the highway. Shattered glass and pieces of steel and fiberglass littered the pavement. The smell of gasoline mixed with the stench of burned flesh.

Frank muttered something, but it was lost beneath the noise of the crowd.

"What'd you say?" I asked.

"There's one more person who ain't going home tonight."

I checked my watch—9:30 p.m. sharp. On a normal night, Terri and I would have finished dinner, talked about our days, and would now be climbing into bed together. We'd be reading books, or watching television, or making love. An hour from now, we'd go to sleep.

On a normal night.

Which this wasn't.

I needed to get home to her. Needed to feel her in my arms, to smell her hair and breathe in her scent and tell her that I loved her. It was very important that I tell her. I said it several times a day, but after years of marriage I didn't really think about it anymore—didn't consider the truth behind the words. Saying "I love you" had become a habit. I needed to let her know that it did still mean something to me, and that I did still love her. I loved her so much it hurt. Something swelled up inside my chest.

"Come on," I said. "We're halfway home."

"Wait," Charlie called, pointing back the way we'd come. "Look at that."

Red lights flashed at the bottom of the hill and slowly came towards us. An ambulance. When the driver turned on the siren my spirits soared.

But they plummeted again when we saw what happened next.

The crowd surged towards the ambulance, swarming it from all sides. They clawed at the doors, crying out for help, begging for medical assistance. The driver laid on the horn and the siren wailed, but the mob kept coming. The ambulance slowed to a crawl, and continued rolling forward, tires crunching a discarded soda can. When it became clear that the paramedics had no intention of stopping, the throng grew angry and then violent. They stood in front of the vehicle, blocking the lanes and preventing it from moving forward. Some people pounded on the windows and several jumped onto the hood, hammering at the windshield with their fists. Another guy climbed up on the roof and jumped up and down. Inside, the eyes of the driver and passenger grew wide. They laid on the horn again as the ambulance rocked back and forth.

"I don't believe this shit," Frank said. "They're gonna tip it over."

"They can't," Charlie said. "They wouldn't."

And then they did. A few unlucky people were crushed beneath the ambulance as the rest of the mob pushed it over onto its side, their shrieks lost beneath the roar of the crowd. One man clambered onto the still-rocking vehicle's side and danced. Enraged rioters smashed the driver's window and pulled the screaming paramedic from his seat. Blood streamed from a gash on his forehead. Struggling, he called out for help, and then disappeared in a swarm of clubs and fists. Flesh struck flesh. The sound of the blows was sickening.

I watched, unable to tear my eyes away. It was horrifying but I had to see.

"We should do something," Charlie whispered. "That poor man."

Frank shook his head. "You kidding? I ain't going down there. Fucking suicide."

The second paramedic was pulled from the vehicle and thrown onto the road. The rioters began kicking him. I heard his bones snap and, despite my shock, was surprised how loud the noise of breaking ribs actually was. He coughed blood, tried to cry out, and then a boot connected with his mouth, shredding his lips. His teeth flew from his mouth like popcorn from an open popper. The injured man raised his arms to cover his head, and the crowd fell on him.

Another rioter dashed forward with a bottle in his hand. A burning rag was stuffed into the neck, and I smelled gasoline.

"Get the fuck back," Frank warned us.

We retreated a few steps. There was a whoosh, and then the ambulance burst into flames. The rioters cheered. Then, looking for a new source on which to focus their rage, the crowd turned on each other. It looked like the world's biggest mosh pit. People fell, pushed or punched, and were then stomped on by those still standing, or weaving around and over and under the parked cars. Windshields and teeth shattered. Tires and stomachs ruptured. Oil and blood flowed. A gunshot rang out, followed by another.

Then, as one, the rioters surged towards us, a single entity composed of fists and angry faces and makeshift weapons.

"Let's go." I grabbed Charlie's arm.

He stumbled forward, his gaze locked on the crowd. "This can't be happening. Society doesn't behave like this."

"What planet you been living on?" Frank snorted, breaking into a trot. "This is exactly how society behaves. Always has."

The violence drew closer.

"Always will," Frank continued. "Especially now. You said it yourself. It wasn't the skinheads that hung that child molester. It was everyday people—people like this."

"Come on," I urged them both.

Exhausted, we ran.

7

An unmoving, naked woman was sprawled out on her back in the middle of the highway at Exit 25. There were twigs and leaves in her hair and gravel embedded in her face. I assumed she had been raped. She was definitely dead. I'd never seen so much blood. Her throat was cut, her nipples, nose and ears sliced off, and her eyes gouged out. She was young and, despite the horrific mutilation, she was beautiful—even in death.

Frank and I both tried our cell phones again, but there was still no service. Meanwhile, after he'd thrown up again, Charlie stripped off his shirt and laid it over the dead woman's face. Then he stood up again, and tucked his undershirt into his pants.

"What are you doing?" I asked.

"Covering her up," he replied. "It seems wrong, leaving her out here like this. Don't want the animals getting at her."

Frank grunted. "Looks like they already did."

I stared at the young woman's body, her upper half now concealed beneath Charlie's shirt. There was a dark purple bruise on her blood-caked thigh, next to a small tattoo of a dolphin jumping through a peace symbol. More blood pooled between her legs. She'd been somebody's daughter, maybe someone's girlfriend or fiancée. She'd been alive. Had hopes and dreams. Now she was fodder. Road kill. Another unlucky casualty, left behind in the dark and never going home again. I wondered who was waiting for her at home. Was there somebody who missed her, or had they disappeared?

Unable to tear my eyes away, I glanced at the damage between her legs. The space between them was no longer recognizable as a part of human anatomy, and I quickly turned my head.

Frank was right. The animals were on the loose tonight, hunting in packs.

I thought of Terri, home alone and probably scared to death.

"I'm coming, honey," I whispered. "Just a little while longer and I'll be home."

Charlie looked at me. "You say something?"

"Nothing. Just tired."

We walked on. A burning car lit the highway. We made sure to give it a wide berth.

An hour later, we saw flames burning several miles ahead of us. It looked like the entire horizon was on fire, just like the other horizon behind us where the city still burned.

Frank pointed. "What the hell's that?"

"I don't know," I said, shrugging. "Forest fire, maybe? That's Exit 26, and there's nothing around there but fields and woods."

As we got closer, we realized that we'd have to walk around, because Exit 26 was gone. The off-ramp, highway and fields on both sides had been obliterated in a plane crash. A section of fuselage jutted up from the mud, its sides scorched and blackened. Smoking wreckage and bodies were scattered throughout the area; it was like walking into a slaughterhouse. The stench of burning jet fuel and oil and flesh grew thick as we approached it.

Frank gaped. "My God . . ."

Charlie coughed. "Wonder what brought it down?"

"Maybe the pilot disappeared," I said. "And the co-pilot."

"Don't they got those auto-pilot things?" Frank wheezed.

My eyes began to sting. I breathed through my mouth to avoid the smell.

"Sure." I wiped the water from my eyes. "But you've still got to have somebody to land the plane."

We cut through the woods, avoiding the sections that were on fire, and came out onto Old York Road, which ran alongside the interstate from Harrisburg to Baltimore. The road was quiet and deserted, free of abandoned or wrecked cars. It was darker here. No houses, businesses or even a traffic light. An owl called out from a tree limb, and a rabbit darted through the undergrowth along the bank. Somewhere in the night, a dog howled. The surrounding forest blocked out the moonlight and the glow from the fires on the nearby highway, but we could still smell the smoke and I wondered if the stench had gotten into our clothes. Then I noticed that the wind had changed direction and was blowing it through the trees. We started down the road and rounded a curve.

"Shit," Frank said. "We should have walked this way to begin with, instead of sticking to 83. There's no traffic at all."

Charlie stopped and pointed. "Except for him."

A county police car sat on the side of the road, the driver's door hanging open. A young, baby-faced cop sat behind the wheel, his head in his hands. He looked up as we approached. His eyes were bloodshot and his face pale.

"Let me guess," he sighed. "You called 911 and nobody answered."

His voice sounded tired. Hollow. Beaten.

"No," Charlie answered. "We were just—"

"Because nobody's at the call center," the cop interrupted. "Some of them went missing, and the others went home soon after. We were routing calls through Baltimore, but then that call center went off-line, too. We don't even have a dispatcher answering the switchboard tonight. Cheryl and Maggie were supposed to start their shift at six and neither one of them came in. I can't get in touch with anybody."

We nodded in commiseration, unsure of how to respond.

Something squelched under my foot. I looked down and saw that I was standing in a puddle of vomit. Now I knew why the cop had his door open. I stepped back and wiped my heel on the grass.

Charlie cleared his throat. "You don't have a partner?"

The cop's voice was monotone. "No, I'm all alone out here. All alone . . ."

"Seems to be a lot of that tonight," Frank said.

The cop ignored the comment. "You guys come from the interstate?"

"From the plane crash?" Frank pointed back the way we'd come.

The cop nodded.

"Yeah, we cut around it," Frank said. "The fire's spreading, though. Any idea when the firemen will get there?"

"I was the only person to respond," the cop said. "Nobody else showed up. No fire departments. No EMTs or NTSB investigators. Or the TSA. No Feds. Just me. Where the hell is everybody? Even with dispatch out, you'd think they'd be patrolling."

"That's what we've been wondering," I told him. "It's like this everywhere."

"Any of you guys got a cell phone? I thought about calling some of the other officers, but I don't have a phone and the pay phones aren't working. Nobody is answering their radios, except for Simmons and all he did was scream."

I shook my head. "Cell phones are out, too. I've been trying to call my wife."

A tear ran down his cheek, and his face crumbled. "There were parts of people hanging in the trees…intestines and stuff. I stepped on somebody's face. It was lying in the mud. Just their face—I don't know where the rest of them was."

He reached in the glove compartment, pulled out a tissue, and blew his nose.

"There was a little girl, lying on the ground. I—I thought she was alive. I grabbed her arm, to pull her up, and it… came off."

"It'll be okay," Charlie said.

"Her fucking arm came off in my fucking hands!"

Charlie stepped closer. "Listen, I know you've had a hell of an evening. We all have. But there's nothing you can do for them now."

The cop frowned. "Yeah, I know. I drove over here to escape the smell. It's in my clothes and my hair. Can't get away from it. I've just been sitting here, waiting. Not sure what to do next."

Charlie held his hands out, pleading. "Could you give us a ride? We're trying to get home. Just over the border."

"Yeah," Frank said. "We've been walking all night. A ride would be great. We'd appreciate the hell out of it."

The distraught man buried his face in his hands again

and shook his head.

"I can't. Not until somebody else shows up. I'm all that's left. You see?"

Frank tried again. "But nobody is going to show up. They'd have been here by now. It's like this everywhere. You said so yourself. Nobody is answering the emergency calls."

"All the more reason then." The officer blew his nose again, and then sat up straight. "It's my job. To serve and protect."

"We'll pay you," I offered in desperation, pulling out my wallet. I opened it, and a picture of Terri smiled at me from behind the plastic sleeve. "I've got sixty bucks."

"Sorry, guys," the cop said. "Really, I am. I'd like to help you. But I can't. I've got to stay."

Charlie and Frank both checked their pockets. I stared at Terri's picture.

"I've got forty," Charlie said. "Frank?"

"Thirty-seven. How about it, Officer? That's almost one hundred and forty bucks."

"And," I added, "I can write you a check for more when we get there."

He paused, and I thought that maybe we'd convinced him. But then he sighed.

"I'm sorry. I'm just going to stay here."

"But why?" I asked, frustrated.

"I'm afraid to go back out there. Afraid of what I'll see. Good luck. Hope you make it home safe."

We didn't argue with him. Instead, we started off again. I cast one glance over my shoulder and he was still sitting there, slumped behind the wheel and crying. His sobs echoed through the night.

It was a lonely sound.

I knew how he felt. I'd missed my wife during the entire journey, but at that moment, it became a solid, tangible thing, swelling deep inside my gut and threatening to explode. My eyes started watering again, and this time it had nothing to do with smoke or fumes. My lips felt numb.

"Thanks, guys," I said, my voice cracking.

Charlie tilted his head from side to side, cracking his neck. "For what?"

"For coming along with me. For not letting me do this alone."

"Safety in numbers, remember?" Charlie winked. "And besides, this is just an extension of our carpool."

"And I needed the exercise." Frank grinned. "Doctor's always on me to do more walking. Well, he got his fucking wish."

His laughter was infectious. We walked together, side by side down the center of the road, and when the darkness swallowed us up, we didn't notice.

8

We reached Hereford, which would have been Exit 27 had we stayed on the interstate. It was a small town, no industries or shopping centers, and only a single bar. The streets were empty, no traffic or pedestrians. Televisions flickered in the windows of some of the homes, but many more were dark and lifeless. Everything looked yellow in the sodium lights that lined the sidewalk.

"I don't know about you guys," Frank wheezed, "but I need something to drink."

His face was as pale as cottage cheese, and his clothing was completely drenched with sweat.

"You okay?" I asked, concerned. "You don't look so good."

"Don't feel so good, either, to be honest. I'm too old for this shit."

"We can stop," I offered. "Take a break?"

Frank shook his head stubbornly. "I'll be okay soon as we find something to drink. I've never gone this long without a beer. Must be withdrawal."

He smiled, trying to laugh it off, but I could see that he was serious.

"Yeah," Charlie agreed. "I'm thirsty, too. Don't know about a beer, but I'd kill for a bottle of water right now."

The Exxon gas station and convenience store was still open, so we stopped there. A bell rang as we walked through the door and the lights were on inside, but there was nobody behind the counter.

Charlie cupped his hands around his mouth. "Hello?"

The fluorescent lights hummed softly in the silence. In the back room, the air compressor kicked on, making sure the soda and milk aisle stayed refrigerated.

"Hey," Charlie yelled again. "Anybody home? You got customers!"

"It's deserted," Frank said. "Maybe the clerk vanished with everyone else."

Something didn't feel right to me, but I couldn't put my finger on it. The compressor suddenly shut itself off. My ears rang in the silence. I sniffed the air and caught a faint trace of cordite.

"Doesn't look like they have a public restroom," Frank observed.

"Maybe they're in the back, using the crapper."

"Screw it," Charlie said. "Let's just take what we need and go."

I started to protest, but he cut me off.

"We'll leave our money on the counter, Steve. That way we're not stealing."

Frank frowned. "It smells like gun smoke in here, don't it?"

I nodded. "I smelled it, too, but I thought it was just me."

Charlie headed down one of the aisles and grabbed a bag of potato chips.

"Hello," I called out. "Anybody here?"

A low moan answered me. We glanced at each other, surprised.

"Behind the counter," Frank whispered.

We ran to the register, and looked over the counter. A Filipino man lay on the floor. He'd been shot in the chest. Blood leaked from the corner of his mouth and pooled beneath him on the tiles. His eyes were open, staring at us in alarm. He coughed, spraying the lottery ticket machine with tiny flecks of red.

"Charlie," I shouted, leaping over the counter. "Call 911. Frank—check in the back room. See if you can find blankets or something."

The manager (he had a name tag that said his name was 'LOPEZ' and he was the 'MANAGER') looked up at me and tried to speak. More blood spilled from his lips. He was obviously in shock. His skin had the color of paste and was cold and clammy to the touch.

"Shhh," I quieted him. "Don't move. We're gonna help you."

Lopez the manager raised his head and whispered into my ear, spattering my shoulder with blood.

"Maraming salamat . . . kaibigan."

I didn't understand, but I smiled, trying to look confident and reassuring and feeling anything but.

"Fuck!" Charlie yelled. "Steve, 911 isn't answering!"

"Keep trying. This guy's lost a lot of blood. We've got to get him help, fast!"

"I'm trying." Charlie hung up the store phone. "It's just like that cop said. Nobody's there to answer the call."

I slapped my head, frustrated. In my panic, I'd forgotten about that. Then a thought occurred to me.

"Do you think you could make it back to that cop?" I asked Charlie.

"Maraming salamat," the man on the floor repeated.

"What'd he say?" Charlie asked me.

"I don't know. Did you—"

Thunder crashed, cutting me off. Then it roared again. On the floor, Lopez flinched and squeezed my hand. His expression was terrified.

That's not thunder, I thought. *Somebody's shooting . . .*

A third gunshot rang out, echoing through the store. I felt the concussion vibrating in my chest. My ears felt like they'd suddenly closed up. Charlie and I both jumped and the manager began to whimper.

"The back room," Charlie whispered.

My ears were still ringing and I had to strain to hear him.

"What do we do?" Charlie asked.

I jumped up. "Frank? FRANK!"

He hollered back. His voice sounded weak, and in pain. "Steve . . . Charlie . . . Run!"

Before we could do anything, the door to the back room flew open and two skinheads stormed out. Both wore tight blue jeans, black combat boots and leather jackets with patches sewn on the front that said, 'Eastern Hammer.' My stomach fluttered. The Eastern Hammer skinheads were notorious in the mid-Atlantic portion of the East Coast, especially in Delaware, Pennsylvania and Maryland. Their headquarters was supposedly in nearby Red Lion. They'd been accused of and—in some cases—tried and convicted of a number of hate crimes, including murder. Supposedly, they were linked to the Sons of the Constitution militia group that was based down south.

I thought back to the Thornton Mill Road overpass. It seemed like years ago, but it had only been a few hours. The child molester, swinging from a noose, his shit splattered all over the highway. Skinheads, they'd told us. Skinheads had killed him. Charlie had been skeptical. I wondered what he thought now. I risked a glance in his direction. His eyes were wide. Then I looked back at the two youths. The tall one had a forehead like a caveman, his brow protruding a half-inch from the rest of his face. The shorter of the two had a long, pink scar on his right cheek and clutched a still-smoking pistol in his hand.

"Get down, you motherfuckers," the taller one shouted. "On the floor, right now!"

"We don't want any trouble," Charlie said. "We were just—"

"Fucking do it," the other one, Scar-face, spat, motioning with the gun. "If I have to say it again, I will waste your ass."

I held my hands out in front of me, and noticed Lopez the manager's blood was all over them. I must have stepped in it, too, because the soles of my shoes seemed stuck to the floor.

"Steve . . ."

"Are you fucking deaf?" Scar-face glared at Charlie. "I told you to—"

Charlie ducked, sprinting for the door. The skinhead fired as the door swung open. Charlie darted through. Glass shattered. The door buzzer rang, almost drowned out by the gunshot. And then Charlie sped across the parking lot and was gone—vanished into the night.

The tall one nodded at his companion. "Go get the fucker, Skink."

So Scar-face had a name.

"He ain't gonna do shit, Al," Skink said. "Cops are busy elsewhere."

Skink and Al. Even their names seemed surreal.

The tall one, Al, spit on the floor. "I said go after him, goddamn it!"

"What about this guy?" Skink pointed at me.

Al smiled. "I'll take care of him."

Cursing, Skink ran after Charlie, his boots crunching on the fragments of broken glass.

Al glowered at me. "Come out from around there, shit-head. Slowly."

"Look," I said. "We don't—"

"SHUT THE FUCK UP AND MOVE!"

Too afraid to open my mouth, I did as he said, stepping over the manager's body and almost slipping in his blood. Lopez's eyes were open, but I couldn't tell if he was still alive. I wondered what had happened to Frank and feared the worst. I crept out from behind the counter, my hands still in the air, and left bloody footprints on the floor.

Well, I thought, *I guess that guy Tony was right and Charlie was wrong. There really are murderous skinheads running around tonight.*

I wondered if these were the same ones who'd apparently hung the child molester from the overpass. The one in front of me, Al, was young—maybe in his early twenties. He looked nervous, but angry. His sloped brow creased in frustration.

The thug studied my face. "You got one ugly fucking nose, you know that?"

"S-so?" I cringed at the tremor in my voice. I sounded anything but brave.

"Jews got noses like that." He cocked his head. "You a kike?"

"No," I lied. My voice was steadier this time. My fear was slowly being replaced with anger. Believe it or not, this was the first time in my life that someone had ever called me a kike to my face. I didn't like how it felt.

"What's your name?" Al demanded.

"Steve." I took another step towards him. "What's yours? I mean, I know your name is Al, but what's the rest?"

I realized I was babbling, but couldn't seem to stop. My voice rose in pitch.

He reached inside his coat and pulled out a knife. "Don't you worry about my fucking name. I'm asking the questions. Get over here."

I glanced around for a weapon, for anything to defend myself with. The cash register, the lottery and credit card machines, a display rack of candy bars. Nothing.

"Hey," Al snarled. "I see you. You're checking out the register. You *are* a fucking Jew, ain't you? Worrying about the money."

I inched closer. "You shot the manager."

"No, I didn't. Skink did."

"How about our friend? He went in the back. Did you kill him, too?"

Al grew angrier. "I'll cut your fucking throat if you don't move faster and do what the fuck I tell you."

"You'll do no such thing," said a man's voice from behind me.

I froze. So did the skinhead. He stared over my shoulder, his eyes narrowing. I thought I recognized the voice. It sounded vaguely familiar. The temperature inside the store suddenly dropped. I saw my breath in the air, drifting like fog. In the back, near the pet food section, the fluorescent bulbs exploded. The rest of the lights grew brighter. I heard the electricity surging through them. The hair on my arms and head stood up and static crackled across my skin.

"He is one of God's chosen," said the voice. "One of the one hundred and forty-four thousand spoken of by John the apostle in the Book of Revelation. He is a saint of the tribulation, and he has many miles to go before he dies. It will not be by your hand, Albert Nicholas, nor will it be tonight."

Al was visibly startled. "How the fuck do you know my name?"

"I know everything."

I wondered whom the new arrival was, and if they were friend or foe, and what the hell they were talking about. What was it he'd said about me? I was a saint of what? I focused on the voice, trying desperately to figure out where I'd heard it before. But I didn't dare turn around.

"Get your ass in here, nigger," the skinhead snarled. "Or I'll cut you, too."

"Cut me?" My savior, who judging by the skinhead's reaction was black, laughed. "Think again, Son of Cain. Not with that you won't."

"What? You don't believe me, fucker? Look at the size of this blade."

The skinhead glanced at his knife. I did, too.

We both screamed at the same time.

His weapon was no longer a knife. Instead, he now clutched a live, thrashing snake. It was about twelve inches long and had brown and yellow scales and beady black eyes. Its tongue flicked across his knuckles and the tail coiled around his wrist. The creature's head weaved from side to side and then darted downward. It sank its fangs into the flesh between Al's thumb and index finger.

"Fuck!" Shrieking, Al ripped the serpent loose and flung it across the store.

I watched it twist and sail through the air and crash into a junk food display, sending bags of potato chips flying. When I looked back at Al, I screamed again.

Al was gone. A white, crystalline statue stared back at me instead, a statue that looked an awful lot like him. Powdery residue fell from its shoulders.

"No harm shall come to you," the voice whispered behind me, and I finally recognized it. The voice was that of Gabriel, the black guy from the crash site. The one wearing the tie with a cross on it who'd caught me when I passed out.

I spun around. The store was empty. Gabriel was nowhere to be seen.

"I know it's you," I called. "Gabriel? Are you following us?"

Silence.

"Gabriel? Thanks for the help. That's twice today."

The temperature inside the store returned to normal. I jumped when the compressor switched itself back on.

"Come on out, man."

Gabriel didn't reply. Outside, through the broken glass in the door, I saw a lone car cruising slowly up the street. One of its headlights was out.

"This Phantom Stranger shit is getting old, Gabriel."

I turned back to the statue of Al. Hesitantly I reached out and touched the coarse, white substance. Then I brought my fingertips to my mouth and tasted.

Salt. The skinhead had been turned into a pillar of salt.

"Holy shit . . ."

I backed away from the statue. Salt granules crunched beneath my feet. I checked the aisles, but they were empty. There was no sign of Gabriel—if he'd even been here. I felt a little part of my mind slip away and tried to get a grip. Last thing I needed to do now was lose it. I had to get home to Terri. What had just happened couldn't have happened. Knives didn't turn into snakes and skinheads definitely didn't turn into pillars of salt.

And half the human race didn't vanish in the blink of an eye, either . . .

Looking around the store, I saw the snake's tail disappearing beneath the coolers, and I decided that it was all very real after all.

Biblical, in fact.

I checked on the manager, but he had no pulse. His skin was cold. His eyes stared sightlessly. I reached out to close them, but couldn't bring myself to touch them. Eventually, I closed my own eyes and just did it.

Then I remembered Frank.

"Fuck!"

Being confronted by Al and Skink, Charlie's fleeing, and everything else that had happened after it had made me forget all about Frank. I cursed my stupidity. He'd called out after the gunshots. Was he okay?

I ran into the back room and found him lying dead on a stack of skids. His glassy eyes gazed at the ceiling and a thin line of blood trickled from his open mouth. There was more blood on his shirt; so much, in fact, that I couldn't figure out where he'd been shot.

"I'm sorry, Frank. I am so sorry, man."

He hadn't deserved this. He was a good guy. He'd joked and laughed for most of our walk, even though he seemed sad underneath it all. Well, of course he'd seemed sad. Still carrying a torch for his ex-wife—it was apparent to strangers like us even if he was oblivious to it himself. No kids or even a beloved pet waiting at home. The only thing Frank looked forward to was the next beer. And now he wouldn't even have that. Even though I'd only known him for an evening, it felt like I'd lost a good friend. I tried to remember things about him, and was surprised by how little I actually knew. I had to think about it for a minute before I could even remember his last name. Some eulogy. It wasn't fair, Frank dying like this, gunned down so senselessly by two racist scumbags. All he'd wanted to do was go home.

Maybe now he had.

Frank's blood was on my hands, literally and figuratively. I reached out to shut his eyes, swallowing the same revulsion I'd felt when doing the same for Lopez.

After closing Frank's eyes, I pulled out my cell phone and attempted to call 911 again. At the very least I should report what had happened. But in truth, after what the cop had told us, I didn't even expect to get a signal, so imagine my surprise when I saw that the phone showed five bars.

Immediately, I forgot about calling the authorities, and instead dialed home. The phone rang, and it was the sweetest sound I've ever heard.

"Yes! Come on, Terri. Pick up. Oh, pick it up."

It rang again.

"Come on, sweetie, be home."

A third ring. A fourth.

"Pick up, pick up, pick up . . ."

Five more rings.

"Answer the goddamn phone!"

It rang three more times before our answering machine finally picked up. I listened to my own voice telling me that Steve and Terri weren't home right now and to leave a message at the beep.

"Terri, it's me. I'm okay. If you're there, pick up the phone! Something's happened, and Craig is missing and people are dead, but I'm okay. Are you there? Terri? Pick up! Pi—"

The machine beeped again, indicating that it was done recording. A recorded voice told me that the mailbox was full.

"Goddamn it!"

I threw the cell phone across the room, and stalked back out to the front of the store. On my way out, I noticed a small, wooden plaque hanging on the wall, discreetly hidden from the view of customers. I studied it. It was some kind of poem, one I wasn't familiar with, obviously of Christian origin. It was called 'Footprints' and was attributed to an unknown author.

One night, the poem began, *a man had a dream. He dreamed he was walking along the beach with the Lord. Across the sky flashed scenes from his life. For each scene, he noticed two sets of footprints in the sand; one belonging to him, and the other to the Lord. When the last scene of his life flashed before him, he looked back at the footprints in the sand. He noticed that many times along the path of his life there was only one set of footprints. He also noticed that it happened at the very lowest and saddest times in his life. This really bothered him, and he questioned the Lord about it. "Lord, you said that once I decided to follow you, you'd walk with me all the way. But I have noticed that during the most troublesome times in my life, there is only one set of footprints. I don't understand why, when I needed you most, you would leave me." The Lord replied, "My son, my precious child, I love you and I would never leave you. During your times of trial and suffering, when you see only one set of footprints, it was then that I carried you."*

I repeated the last line out loud, and then I started shaking. My hands curled into fists. Enraged, I ripped the plaque from the wall and threw it across the store.

"Fuck you," I shouted. "Are you walking with me now? Are you carrying me? Why did you do this to us? What's the point? Were you really behind it? So this is the Rapture, huh? You called your followers home and left us sinners behind. Why? Because Charlie was gay? Because I'm a Jew? Because Frank didn't believe in you anymore? Bastard!"

I waited for a divine lightning bolt to come down and strike me, but it didn't. There was no thunder. The lights didn't even flicker.

"I'll walk my path alone," I whispered, thinking of Gabriel.

It had gotten darker outside—which seemed impossible given what time of night it was. I walked out of the store, and looked around for Charlie, Skink or the mysterious Gabriel, but there was no sign of them. I hoped that Charlie was okay, that he'd gotten away or had enough sense to hide. Maybe he'd find some help, find the cop, and come back. Maybe not. It didn't matter. He was my friend, but I couldn't wait for him. Not anymore.

Craig was missing, along with several million other people. Hector and Frank were dead; Frank gunned down by skinheads and Hector with a pipe through his face. Charlie was gone, and Skink was still on the loose. And if all of this wasn't enough, a weird black guy was following me up the highway, changing knives into snakes and skinheads into pillars of salt.

And Terri wasn't answering the phone.

I headed north, sticking to the side of the road. I'd gone about a half-mile when I found Charlie. He was lying in a ditch. He'd been shot twice, in the stomach and the lower back. Despite his wounds, he was still alive. Nearby, in the driveway of a darkened house, stood another pillar of salt. Skink.

"Hey." Charlie coughed, grimacing. "What took you so long?"

"Jesus Christ." I knelt beside him, staring at the damage. "Don't try to move, man."

He grinned. "Couldn't move if I wanted to. I can't feel anything below my neck. Kind of glad for that, to be honest."

He started to cry. I patted him.

"Oh Charlie…"

"Don't worry. Like I said, I can't feel a thing."

"What happened?"

He stopped crying and coughed again. His chest rattled and black fluid leaked from the corners of his mouth.

"That fucker came after me. Figured I'd run this way and lose him, then double around back and check on you and Frank. How is he?"

I shook my head.

"Damn," Charlie croaked. "He turned out to be an okay guy. I liked him."

"Charlie, what happened to the skinhead? Did you see? Was it Gabriel?"

His eyes clouded. "Who?"

"Gabriel. The guy from the wreck. The one who caught me."

Charlie smiled. If he heard my question, he gave no indication. Instead, he reached out and clasped my hand.

"Got a joke for you. A Jew, a Polack, and a homo are on their way home. Who gets there first?"

I squeezed his hand. "Charlie, don't. Listen to me, man. I'm gonna get help."

"Go find Terri, man. Get home."

"I can't just leave you here."

"Bet I get home before you do."

His chest rose then fell. It did not rise again.

I cried then, shuddering as huge, overwhelming sobs wracked my body. I leaned over and touched my forehead to my friend's. I cried for Charlie and for Frank, for Hector and Craig and everybody else. I cried for Terri. I cried for myself.

I shuffled north again, still crying. I kept to the side of the road, walking through fields and yards rather than on the pavement itself. When I looked down, I realized I was trekking through mud. I glanced behind me.

There was one set of footprints in the mud. Mine.

I walked on, alone.

9

I continued up York Road for a few miles until the darkness and the silence got to be too much for me. By then, the fires from the plane crash had faded beyond the horizon. Eventually, I cut across the fields and back onto the interstate. There was a steep hill ahead of me, and my leg muscles cramped as I climbed it. Still I pressed forward, gritting my teeth and trying to ignore the pain. It wasn't until I'd reached the top that I realized I was crying again. I wiped my nose on my sleeve, and blinked the tears away.

Another cramp shot up my leg, paralyzing it. Screaming, I collapsed to my knees in the middle of the road. Sharp pebbles jabbed through my pants and I reopened the cuts on my hand, but I didn't care. I knelt there, my blood and tears flowing freely.

I didn't notice the station wagon until it was right behind me. I looked up and shielded my eyes from the headlights' glare. The motor purred softly. The vehicle rolled to a stop just a few feet away. I heard the whir of a power window being lowered.

"Are you okay, son?"

I stood up, wiped my eyes, and approached the driver's side door.

A bald man, probably in his late fifties or early sixties, leaned out the window and smiled at me.

"Are you alright?" he asked again. "Do you need help?"

"I—I need a ride. I'm trying to get home to my wife."

"Where do you live?"

"Shrewsbury. It's the first exit in Pennsylvania."

Smiling, he motioned the passenger door. "Certainly. I pass it every day. Hop in. I'm going as far as Harrisburg."

I rounded the vehicle and opened the door. For a brief second, I had misgivings. After everything else I'd been through tonight, and some of the people I'd met, I wondered if it was smart to climb in a car with a stranger. But the pain in my legs came back, and I thought again of Terri and my unanswered phone call. I got inside, pulled the door shut, and settled into the seat.

The man put the car in gear and pulled away. "Lucky for you I wasn't speeding. I might have run right over you. What were you doing in the middle of the highway?"

I swallowed, trying to catch my breath. "It's been a rough evening."

"Yes." He nodded, staring at the road. "It has indeed."

I covered my mouth with my hand and coughed. My throat felt like it had been rubbed with sandpaper, but the pain in my legs was dissipating now that I was sitting down.

"Are you thirsty?" he asked, sipping from a plastic travel mug. I nodded.

"There's a small cooler behind you. I keep drinks in the car so I don't have to stop. Saves me money and time. Help yourself. There should be some bottles of water inside, or soda if you prefer."

"Thanks." I turned and found the cooler, and got a bottle out. The water was ice cold and refreshing, and soothed my raw throat. "I really appreciate this."

"My pleasure." He stuck out his right hand. "Reverend Phillip Brady."

"Steve Leiberman. Thanks again, Reverend. Can I offer you some gas money or something?"

"You can offer it, but I won't accept. It's really no problem. I'm going right by your exit. I volunteer in one of the soup kitchens down in Baltimore, and commute from Harrisburg. I come this way every day."

I whistled in appreciation. "That's a long drive."

"It's what the Lord wants."

"What God wants, God gets?"

He frowned slightly. "That's not quite how I'd put it, but I suppose so. It's what God expects of me."

I laughed, long and hard. The preacher looked shocked,

and immediately, I felt embarrassed and worried that I'd offended him.

"Sorry, Reverend. I'm not laughing at you. It's just, with all that's happened today, all the disappearances, I was pretty much convinced that the Rapture had occurred. Seriously. If you could have seen some of the things I've seen tonight... I was really starting to get scared. But now, after meeting you, I know otherwise. It's not the Rapture. Whatever it was that happened today, whatever took all those people, it wasn't that."

"Actually, I think it *was* the Rapture."

"But you're still here and you're a man of God. Look, I'm Jewish and I don't pretend to understand the whole thing, but my wife and her parents were Christian, too. I thought that when the Rapture occurred, all the Christians were called up to Heaven or something? That's what my in-laws always said."

"Not at all. In fact, I imagine that this Sunday the churches around the world will be filled to capacity. We'll see more people in church than ever before."

"But that doesn't make sense."

"Being a Christian isn't enough. There are still plenty of believers who've been left behind. Just like myself."

I shook my head. "I don't understand."

"How about a quick lesson?"

"Okay." I glanced out the window and saw the exit for Gunpowder Falls flash past. Had I been on foot, it would have taken me another hour to reach it. Instead, it had taken five minutes. The last thing I wanted was a sermon, but I'd sit through one if it got me home to Terri sooner.

Reverend Brady took another sip from his travel mug. "'For the Lord himself will come down from Heaven, with a loud command, with the voice of the archangel and with the trumpet call of God, and we who are still alive will be caught up together in the clouds to meet the Lord in the air. And so we will be with the Lord forever.'"

I didn't respond. I wanted answers, not Bible quotes.

"Sorry," the Reverend apologized, as if reading my mind. "That's from Thessalonians. Talking about a great event. The Rapture is that event—God's calling up millions of His

believers to Heaven. It's a prelude to the Second Coming of
Christ, when Jesus comes back to rule over all. I'm sure that,
like everyone else, you heard the trumpet blast that preceded
today's events?"

I nodded. "That's really what it was?"

"In First Corinthians, the apostle Paul states that in the
twinkling of an eye, the last trumpet will sound and the
believers in Christ will be called home. That's what happened
today. Those who were born again, meaning they'd accepted
Christ as their Lord and Savior, disappeared."

"Where did they go?"

"Heaven."

"But not you. And I saw others today, too: priests and
nuns and people with those stupid Jesus-fish bumper stickers.
We saw a guy preaching on the hood of his car, right in the
middle of the interstate. If God took all of his followers
home, why did He leave people like you behind? Aren't you
pissed off about it?"

"No, I'm not angry." Reverend Brady smiled sadly. "But
you're absolutely right. I am still here. It's my fault. And that
breaks my heart, because I know what's coming next. I know
what the next seven years will bring."

"I still don't understand. If this is the Rapture, then why
aren't you among the missing?"

"Because I lacked belief. One of the most famous verses
in the Bible is, 'For God so loved the world, that He gave His
only begotten Son; that whosoever believes in Him shall not
perish, but have eternal life.' Jesus died for our sins, but in
the last few years, I've lost touch with Him."

"You didn't believe?"

"No," he whispered. "I didn't. When you're a pastor,
whether you want to or not, you become the clearinghouse
for your congregation's gossip. Every single day, I'd overhear
the worst—their darkest secrets, the things they didn't
think anybody else knew. I was exposed to their most base,
animalistic natures. Adultery. Abuse. Sexual depravity. Drug
addiction and alcoholism. Gambling. Theft and deception.
One of our lay speakers embezzled over thirty-thousand
dollars from his employer. Our church secretary poisoned

her neighbor's dog because it wouldn't stop barking. Our youth pastor was engaging in a sexual relationship with his own fourteen-year old daughter."

"And they told you all this?"

He shrugged. "Sometimes. Often I'd hear it from others. But sometimes they'd tell me themselves. Unlike the Catholic Church we don't require confession, but they'd confess to me anyway, looking for guidance. Looking for somebody to assure them it was okay, that God still loved them. And I'd do that. I'd remind them that God forgives all, and they'd promise me they'd do right from now on—and then two months later they'd be right back at it again."

He sighed. The radio played softly. In the soft glow of the dashboard lights, he looked older than I had assumed he was.

"I grew resentful. Not only of them, but of God, too. How was I supposed to be a shepherd, how could I guide them and teach them to live as the Lord wanted, when they filled me with such revulsion? I hated them for it and, eventually, I began to hate God as well. I was just going through the motions. But my congregation was still counting on me. Not all of them were bad people and I couldn't let them down. So I stood up there in the pulpit every Sunday, and I preached the good news, told them about the Lord, and lent them the power of my belief. And all the while, deep down inside, I lacked the faith of my convictions. I didn't believe."

"And here you are," I finished for him.

"Yes, indeed. Here I am. Left behind. God help me—help us all."

"We'll survive," I said. "We'll pick up the pieces, dust ourselves off and move on. We always do. Look at everything the human race has been through. We always bounce back."

He shook his head. "Not this time. The next seven years will quite literally be hell on earth. War. Famine. Earthquakes. Disease. Total chaos."

"Don't we have that now?"

"No, Steve. This is just the beginning. We have those things now, but they pale in comparison to what's coming. This will be a tough time for the tribulation saints."

I gasped.

"What's wrong?" he asked.

"I—something you said just made me think. I heard something similar earlier today."

"How so?"

I told him about all that had transpired. Even with the disappearances, I didn't expect him to believe me when I got to Gabriel and the skinheads turning into salt. But when I'd finished, he simply nodded his head.

"You've been chosen."

I snorted, trying to keep the sarcasm out of my voice. "Chosen for what?"

"Don't scoff. A dynamic new leader is about to arise. People will see him as a great man. He will fix everything, stop the lawlessness and chaos and usher in an era of peace."

"But you said it would be Hell on earth. Wars and famine and all that."

"It's a false peace, and he's anything but a great man. The Bible calls this man Antichrist. He's a descendent of those who destroyed the temple in Jerusalem in 70 A.D. But who he really is, is Satan. The Antichrist will enjoy worldwide popularity. People will love him like no other world leader they've ever known."

"Who is he?"

"I don't know. He has yet to reveal himself. But I'm sure he's already active. We've probably watched him in action for years, and loved him without knowing his true identity. Soon, most likely within a few weeks, he will set up a new one-world government in response to today's events. He'll even bring peace to Israel with the signing of a seven-year agreement."

"Never happen," I said. "There will never be peace in Israel, especially now. And what does this have to do with me anyway? You said I was chosen."

"The signing of the agreement kicks off a seven-year period called the tribulation, and those who receive Jesus as their Lord and Savior after the Rapture are called tribulation saints. Many of them will be Jews, just like you. Revelation talks about the 144,000 Jewish witnesses. These witnesses, the tribulation saints, will be protected supernaturally from the horrors to come. Much like you were today, with your guardian. What did you say his name was?"

"Gabriel," I whispered. He'd mentioned something about the 144,000 as well, when Al the skinhead held me at knifepoint.

"Gabriel the Protector. You do know Gabriel was an angel of the Lord?"

"No," I said. "But I do now."

I tried to get my head around it. I was chosen simply for being Jewish? I didn't even practice my own faith, let alone know the Christian Bible. It all seemed unfair. If this were true, and I was beginning to believe it was, why should I get special protection while others suffered?

We passed the exit for Parkton, and I thought of Charlie. What had he done to deserve all that had happened tonight? He was just trying to get home—same with Frank and Hector and everyone else.

"Why?" I asked. "Why would God do this? He's supposed to be a loving God."

"Yes," Brady said, "and He is a loving God. But he is also a just God. A comedian who I enjoy once said that the God of the Bible had a split personality. In the New Testament, He is a God of love, promising forgiveness to everyone; but in the Old Testament, He is a God of wrath, demanding sacrifices and punishing those who displease him. People often forget that he is both."

I considered telling the preacher just what I thought of that, what I thought of his God—of any deity that would do this to its people. But I kept my mouth shut and watched the mile markers rush by. This man could deliver me almost to my doorstep, so the last thing I wanted to do was offend him. If I did, I'd find myself walking again.

We passed the weigh station at Exit 36, and crossed over the state line. There were three small crosses off the shoulder, set up in remembrance of three teenagers who'd died there months ago in a drunken driving accident. Looking at them, I shivered.

"Pennsylvania." Reverend Brady smiled. "Won't be long now."

I looked up at the road sign.

YOU ARE NOW LEAVING MARYLAND.
WE ENJOYED YOUR VISIT.
PLEASE COME AGAIN.

Please come again . . .
It was a fitting epitaph for the world.

10

We drove on in silence, past the deserted Pennsylvania Welcome Center and a few more scattered car wrecks. I watched the sights flick past, numb to the horrors. A farmhouse burned; no firefighters were on site. A decapitated head lay on the median. A teenage graffiti artist had tagged a billboard without fear of retribution or arrest, because the cops were all busy elsewhere. A large, black crow feasted on a dead dog.

The headlights flashed off a road sign: *Shrewsbury—One Mile*.

"You can just drop me off at the exit ramp," I said.

Reverend Brady looked surprised. "Are you sure? It's not a problem to take you to your front door."

"No, that's okay. I'm sure you've got people to get home to as well."

He slowed down as we approached the exit and stopped at the top of the ramp. He checked the rearview mirror to make sure there was no traffic behind us. There wasn't. The highway was a ghost.

I opened the door, and then offered him my hand. "Look. I don't know how to thank you. Are you sure I can't give you some gas money or something?"

"You can thank me by thinking about what I said." He squeezed my hand. "I hope you find what you're looking for when you get home, Steve."

"I appreciate that. Goodbye, Reverend, and good luck."

"I'll pray for you, and for your wife."

"Thanks."

I started to turn away, but then he called out.

"Steve? Don't lose faith. The journey will be hard, but something wonderful is waiting for you at the end."

I nodded, afraid to speak. Despite the kindness he'd shown me, I felt like screaming at him. The car's window slid closed, and Reverend Brady drove away. I stood there and watched him go until his taillights vanished.

"Gabriel?" I said out loud as I walked down the exit ramp. "You still with me?"

There was no answer, but I wasn't really expecting one. If anything, Gabriel had proven himself to be pretty non-communicative.

"So if the preacher was right, if you're some sort of guardian angel sent to watch over me, then I hope you watched over Terri as well."

In the darkness, a whippoorwill sang out. The grass along the roadside rustled softly in the breeze.

"If not," I said, "there'll be hell to pay."

Then I went home.

11

They were looting the Wal-Mart as I walked past. Surprisingly, the whole thing seemed pretty civil. Locals, people I knew and faces I recognized, filed out of the store carrying everything from food to televisions. They pushed shopping carts filled to overflowing with goods. There was no fighting or shoving. It was eerily calm. Neighbors greeted each other, and helped each other load up their cars and trucks. I heard laughter, saw lovers holding hands, children smiling. The scene was polite and friendly, almost festive. A carnival atmosphere where all that was missing was a Ferris wheel and a few cotton candy vendors. Maybe a trained elephant doing tricks for the kids, as well.

Charlie had been right. We should have taken the abandoned Cadillac when we came across it. Everybody else was doing it, and the Caddy's owner doubtlessly wouldn't have needed it again. Had we commandeered the car, I'd have been home already. We'd all be home. If I'd said yes, Charlie and Frank would still be alive.

There weren't many abandoned cars in town, but there were a lot of dark houses. I wondered how many of their occupants had actually disappeared and how many more were simply hiding inside, hunkered down behind the windowsill, clutching a shotgun in the darkness and waiting for the hordes invading the Wal-Mart to attack.

On one block where the homes were close to one another, a fire had gutted four buildings, stretching from Merle Laughman's antique shop down to Dale Haubner's house. The sidewalks and street were wet and water dripped from the fire hydrant. I assumed that the firefighters here in our community had been less busy than elsewhere. Or maybe they'd just gotten to this one early. Whatever had occurred, they'd managed to save the rest of the block.

The pain in my legs and feet had dissipated during the car ride, and now I had my second wind. The fatigue lessened with each step, and I quickened my pace.

"I'm almost there, Terri. Almost home."

The traffic light blinked yellow at the intersection across from my block. Shattered glass indicated a wreck, but there were no cars in sight. I crossed Main Street, turned right, and walked another few yards.

Then I stood in front of our house. I took a deep breath. The lights were on and I saw the flickering blue glow of the television from the living room window.

"She's here!"

I ran up the stairs of the front porch and my hands shook as I fumbled for my keys. I unlocked the door and barged into the living room. A frazzled-looking newscaster was on television, reporting on what I already knew. The volume was turned up loud.

Terri's spot on the couch was empty, but the cushion where she sat every evening still held her imprint.

"Terri? Honey? I'm home!"

I turned off the television.

"Terri?"

Silence. I was home, but my wife wasn't. I searched the house, hoping against hope, but I knew what I would find. Or wouldn't find.

Terri was missing.

After twenty minutes, I collapsed onto the bed and cried into her pillow. It smelled like Terri, and I breathed in her fading scent. Soon it would be gone, just like her imprint on the sofa cushion. And then there'd be no trace left.

I prayed. I asked for it to be taken back, that the day be rewound and erased. Prayed for a second chance. I prayed for Charlie and Frank and Craig and Hector and all the others. More than anything, I asked for my wife to be returned to me, or to be allowed to go where she was, and again there was no answer. God was deaf, dumb and blind. I pleaded with Gabriel to show himself, but he didn't. The silence was a solid thing. Downstairs, our grandfather clock ticked off the seconds and each one was excruciating.

I lay there all night and continued to pray. My parents would have been so proud of me. Terri and her parents would have been proud, too, because I finally believed in something. Believed in a force beyond Judaism or Christianity or dogma or faith. Believed in something concrete.

Something real.

I prayed as only a God-fearing man can—because God exists. I know that now. God exists, and I fear Him.

I am afraid.

So I pray. I pray every day now, even as things get worse. The preacher was right. The Rapture was just the beginning. And still I pray. I pray for mercy. Pray for forgiveness.

Pray to go home.

It's such a long way and there are many miles left to go.

AFTERWORD

Take The Long Way Home was originally written for an anthology called *On A Pale Horse*. The premise of the anthology was four religious themed, end-of-the-world novellas by four different horror writers—myself, Tim Lebbon, Michael Laimo, and Gord Rollo. Each of us began work on our novellas, and everybody agreed that I should write about the Rapture. Why? At the time, there was a very popular Christian horror series written by Tim LaHaye and Jerry Jenkins called *Left Behind*. The series spanned twelve-books and a subsequent young adult series before giving birth to its first prequel. That prequel, amusingly enough, was called *The Rising*. My own book, *The Rising*, which caused a stir among zombie fans, had been out for about two years at that point. You can imagine the fun that ensued for booksellers. Zombie fans who had read *City of the Dead* and were looking for the previous book picked up something about the Rapture instead, and Christian readers who were expecting more of LaHaye and Jenkins' Biblical adventure got Ob and Frankie and a bunch o' gut-munching zombies.

I originally wanted to call this story *Left Behind*. My attorney said we couldn't be sued for it, and I laughed with glee. But then a friend's more sensible head prevailed, and I changed the title to *Take The Long Way Home*, which is also the title of my favorite Supertramp song. I think I like this title better.

Sadly, despite the best efforts of everyone involved, *On A Pale Horse* fell through. Luckily, *Take The Long Way Home* was published several years ago as a beautiful little limited edition hardcover. Then it was reprinted in my now out of print short story collection *Unhappy Endings*. And now Deadite Press has released this new edition.

The story itself is based on the primarily evangelical interpretation of the Biblical scriptures, specifically the Rapture and how it relates to the Second Coming of Christ. The 144,000 Jews who become Tribulation Saints are a part of this belief.

I was raised by two Irish-American Protestant parents, attended a Methodist church, and was even the president of the church youth group at one point, if you can dig that. My grandparents were Presbyterians, my extended family hardcore Southern Baptists, and I once dated a preacher's daughter. My point is; I was surrounded by religion, specifically Christianity, all through my childhood and teenage years. Readers have commented that my fiction seems to be primarily based on the Christian mythos—well, that's why.

Readers have also said that they see a deep schism; that I often depict God as the ultimate bad guy, and I think that's also a fair assumption. I trace that to adulthood. As a young man, I traveled the world and was exposed to many other religions and alternative ways of thinking. I came to realize that what I was brought up to believe wasn't the whole truth, the big picture, and that there were millions of other people whose ideas and faiths were just as valid and deep and personal.

I've gone through phases: occultism, powwow, paganism, Buddhism, atheism, and finally, agnosticism. At forty-three, I'm no longer sure what I believe, and that bothers me more and more each day. I believe in an afterlife, but I'm not sure that it's Heaven. I believe that there's something more to this world, to this universe, something behind the veil, but I'm not sure that it's God.

Sometimes, it seems like the more I learn, the less I know.

I do know this. I often feel like Steve does at the end of this story. Sometimes, that kid inside of me, the kid who read Marvel comic books and rode his BMX Mongoose and watched *Land of the Lost* and *Six-Million Dollar Man*, and listened to Rush and Ozzy Osbourne—and still made it to church every Sunday, speaks up and lets me know that he's still alive, that this cold, hard, cynical bastard I've become hasn't buried him completely. It is during these times that I remember exactly why I went to church each Sunday.

Fear.

Fear of getting spanked by my parents for not going; fear of not fitting in with my peers (because back then, most of the cool kids did indeed go to church); and most of all, fear of what God would do to me if I didn't.

Fear of God.

I like to think I'm a new world man. I don't think religion should have any place in our schools or government or courts. I think we should reach out to other cultures and ways of life, regardless of whether they believe in our God or their God or any god. In my novel *Terminal*, when Tommy O'Brien rants that religion has fucked this planet up since day one, that's Brian Keene talking. It has. Most of the evils perpetrated by mankind aren't the work of the Devil, but can be traced back to religion; all done in God's name.

I'd like to think I've evolved beyond that. But then that kid inside of me, the one who made sure he sat still during the sermon and paid attention during Sunday school, speaks up, and reminds me of my fear.

I am afraid of God, and therefore, I believe.

I'm afraid not to.

Brian Keene
January 2011

BRIAN KEENE is the author of over twenty-five books, including *Darkness on the Edge of Town, Urban Gothic, Castaways, Kill Whitey, Dark Hollow, Dead Sea, Ghoul* and *The Rising*. He also writes comic books such as *The Last Zombie, Doom Patrol* and *Dead of Night: Devil Slayer*. His work has been translated into German, Spanish, Polish, Italian, French and Taiwanese. Several of his novels and stories have been optioned for film, one of which, *The Ties That Bind*, premiered on DVD in 2009 as a critically-acclaimed independent short. Keene's work has been praised in such diverse places as *The New York Times*, The History Channel, The Howard Stern Show, CNN.com, *Publisher's Weekly, Fangoria Magazine*, and *Rue Morgue Magazine*. Keene lives in Central Pennsylvania. You can communicate with him online at www.briankeene.com, on Facebook at www.facebook.com/pages/Brian-Keene/189077221397 or on Twitter at www.twitter.com/BrianKeene

deadite press

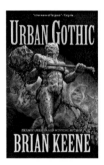

"Urban Gothic" Brian Keene - When their car broke down in a dangerous inner-city neighborhood, Kerri and her friends thought they would find shelter inside an old, dark row home. They thought they would be safe there until help arrived. They were wrong. The residents who live down in the cellar and the tunnels beneath the city are far more dangerous than the streets outside, and they have a very special way of dealing with trespassers. Trapped in a world of darkness, populated by obscene abominations, they will have to fight back if they ever want to see the sun again.

"Jack's Magic Beans" Brian Keene - It happens in a split-second. One moment, customers are happily shopping in the Save-A-Lot grocery store. The next instant, they are transformed into bloodthirsty psychotics, interested only in slaughtering one another and committing unimaginably atrocious and frenzied acts of violent depravity. Deadite Press is proud to bring one of Brian Keene's bleakest and most violent novellas back into print once more. This edition also includes four bonus short stories:

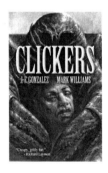

"Clickers" J. F. Gonzalez and Mark Williams- They are the Clickers, giant venomous blood-thirsty crabs from the depths of the sea. The only warning to their rampage of dismemberment and death is the terrible clicking of their claws. But these monsters aren't merely here to ravage and pillage. They are being driven onto land by fear. Something is hunting the Clickers. Something ancient and without mercy. *Clickers* is J. F. Gonzalez and Mark Williams' gore-soaked cult classic tribute to the giant monster B-movies of yesteryear.

"Clickers II" J. F. Gonzalez and Brian Keene- Thousands of Clickers swarm across the entire nation and march inland, slaughtering anyone and anything they come across. But this time the Clickers aren't blindly rushing onto land - they are being led by an intelligence older than civilization itself. A force that wants to take dry land away from the mammals. Those left alive soon realize that they must do everything and anything they can to protect humanity – no matter the cost. *This isn't war, this is extermination.*

"Whargoul" Dave Brockie - It is a beast born in bullets and shrapnel, feeding off of pain, misery, and hard drugs. Cursed to wander the Earth without the hope of death, it is reborn again and again to spread the gospel of hate, abuse, and genocide. But what if it's not the only monster out there? What if there's something worse? From Dave Brockie, the twisted genius behind GWAR, comes a novel about the darkest days of the twentieth century.

"Rock and Roll Reform School Zombies" Bryan Smith - Sex, Death, and Heavy Metal! The Southern Illinois Music Reeducation Center specializes in "de-metaling" – a treatment to cure teens of their metal loving, devil worshiping ways. A program that subjects its prisoners to sexual abuse, torture, and brain-washing. But tonight things get much worse. Tonight the flesh-eating zombies come . . . *Rock and Roll Reform School Zombies* is Bryan Smith's tribute to "Return of the Living Dead" and "The Decline of Western Civilization Part 2: the Metal Years."

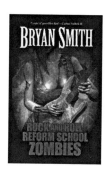

"Brain Cheese Buffet" Edward Lee - collecting nine of Lee's most sought after tales of violence and body fluids. Featuring the Stoker nominated "Mr. Torso," the legendary gross-out piece "The Dritiphilist," the notorious "The McCrath Model SS40-C, Series S," and six more stories to test your gag reflex.
"Edward Lee's writing is fast and mean as a chain saw revved to full-tilt boogie."
 - Jack Ketchum

"Bullet Through Your Face" Edward Lee - No writer is more extreme, perverted, or gross than Edward Lee. His world is one of psychopathic redneck rapists, sex addicted demons, and semen stealing aliens. Brace yourself, the king of splatterspunk is guaranteed to shock, offend, and make you laugh until you vomit.
"Lee pulls no punches."
 - Fangoria

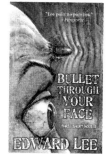

THE VERY BEST IN CULT HORROR

deadite press

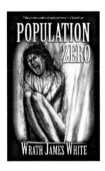

"Population Zero" Wrath James White - An intense sadistic tale of how one man will save the world through sterilization. *Population Zero* is the story of an environmental activist named Todd Hammerstein who is on a mission to save the planet. In just 50 years the population of the planet is expected to double. But not if Todd can help it. From Wrath James White, the celebrated master of sex and splatter, comes a tale of environmentalism, drugs, and genital mutilation.

"Trolley No. 1852" Edward Lee - In 1934, horror writer H.P. Lovecraft is invited to write a story for a subversive underground magazine, all on the condition that a pseudonym will be used. The pay is lofty, and God knows, Lovecraft needs the money. There's just one catch. It has to be a pornographic story . . . The 1852 Club is a bordello unlike any other. Its women are the most beautiful and they will do anything. But there is something else going on at this sex club. In the back rooms monsters are performing vile acts on each other and doors to other dimensions are opening . . .

"Zombies and Shit" Carlton Mellick III - *Battle Royale* meets *Return of the Living Dead* in this post-apocalyptic action adventure. Twenty people wake to find themselves in a boarded-up building in the middle of the zombie wasteland. They soon realize they have been chosen as contestants on a popular reality show called Zombie Survival. Each contestant is given a backpack of supplies and a unique weapon. Their goal: be the first to make it through the zombie-plagued city to the pick-up zone alive. A campy, trashy, punk rock gore fest.

"Slaughterhouse High" Robert Devereaux - It's prom night in the Demented States of America. A place where schools are built with secret passageways, rebellious teens get zippers installed in their mouths and genitals, and once a year one couple is slaughtered and the bits of their bodies are kept as souvenirs. But something's gone terribly wrong when the secret killer starts claiming a far higher body count than usual . . .
"A major talent!" - Poppy Z. Brite

"The Book of a Thousand Sins" Wrath James White - Welcome to a world of Zombie nymphomaniacs, psychopathic deities, voodoo surgery, and murderous priests. Where mutilation sex clubs are in vogue and torture machines are sex toys. No one makes it out alive – not even God himself.
"If Wrath James White doesn't make you cringe, you must be riding in the wrong end of a hearse."
-Jack Ketchum

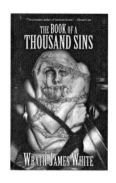

"The Haunter of the Threshold" Edward Lee - There is something very wrong with this backwater town. Suicide notes, magic gems, and haunted cabins await her. Plus the woods are filled with monsters, both human and otherworldly. And then there are the horrible tentacles . . . Soon Hazel is thrown into a battle for her life that will test her sanity and sex drive. The sequel to H.P. Lovecraft's The Haunter of the Dark is Edward Lee's most pornographic novel to date!

"Apeshit" Carlton Mellick III - Friday the 13th meets Visitor Q. Six hipster teens go to a cabin in the woods inhabited by a deformed killer. An incredibly fucked-up parody of B-horror movies with a bizarro slant
"The new gold standard in unstoppable fetus-fucking kill-freakomania . . . Genuine all-meat hardcore horror meets unadulterated Bizarro brainwarp strangeness. The results are beyond jaw-dropping, and fill me with pure, unforgivable joy." - John Skipp

"Super Fetus" Adam Pepper - Try to abort this fetus and he'll kick your ass!
"The story of a self-aware fetus whose morally bankrupt mother is desperately trying to abort him. This darkly humorous novella will surely appall and upset a sizable percentage of people who read it . . . In-your-face, allegorical social commentary."
- BarnesandNoble.com

AVAILABLE FROM AMAZON.COM

Breinigsville, PA USA
28 March 2011
258618BV00003B/51/P